Two red Terminator jackets walked through the gym doors. Inside them were Dabny and his brother Kevin. If Dabny's description is big and scary, his brother is Dabny with twenty extra pounds of muscle and fifty extra pounds of nastiness. When they walked across the gym and stood in front of me, I was a half-degree away from a total meltdown.

"We have to talk about our deal, Stormy."

"Our deal?"

"You know. You pay us a quarter a day and we stay out of your hair. You didn't pay yesterday and said something on the phone about never paying again. That was a mistake, wasn't it?"

I wasn't sure how to answer.

"The last thing I need is another puke-faced seventh grader giving me a hard time." Kevin stepped aside. "He's all yours, bro."

Dabny took two steps forward to get within right hook distance.

"What was it you said last night, Stormy? You called me a fathead, didn't you?"

Other Avon Flare Books by
Martyn Godfrey

CAN YOU TEACH ME TO PICK MY NOSE?

PLEASE REMOVE *Your* ELBOW *From* MY EAR

MARTYN GODFREY

AN AVON  FLARE BOOK

To Tog the Dog

PLEASE REMOVE YOUR ELBOW FROM MY EAR is an original publication of Avon Books. This work has never before appeared in book form.

AVON BOOKS
A division of
The Hearst Corporation
1350 Avenue of the Americas
New York, New York 10019

First Avon Flare Printing: July 1993

AVON FLARE TRADEMARK REG. U.S. PAT. OFF. AND IN OTHER COUNTRIES, MARCA REGISTRADA, HECHO EN U.S.A.

Printed in the U.S.A.

RA 10 9 8 7 6 5 4 3 2 1

1.

A Perfect Clarence

I didn't have any idea how that Tuesday was going to change my life forever. It seemed perfectly normal in every way. I was in my school, Taft Junior High, in Burlington, Vermont. And, as usual, I was being picked on.

This time my tormentor was Pierce Kobel, one half of the dippy Kobel twins and, in my biased opinion, as close to a certified Neanderthal as anyone can get. He'd decided it would be a good idea to pull a *clarence* on me in the middle of gym class.

I was leaning on a floor hockey stick, daydreaming about Loreeta Simpson, the new girl in my seventh grade homeroom, when Pierce snuck up behind me, grabbed my sweatpants, and yanked them down.

A perfect *clarence*.

I stood in my underwear, looking suitably lame, while Pierce and his buddies broke into a chorus of laughter.

"Lose something, Stormy?" Pierce taunted.

"Hey, Sprague, isn't it a little breezy?" his brother Adon added.

Naturally, I was upset. Pierce wasn't a big guy. He didn't intimidate me with his size. So I figured I had two choices. First, and the more sensible, I could pull up my pants and walk away.

Don't give them the thrill of seeing how much they've humiliated you, the little voice in my head reasoned.

Course, I have a hard time listening to that voice. People tease me because I have a habit of saying and doing stupid things.

I wasn't about to disappoint anybody.

For a brief moment, I contemplated a hatchet blow to Pierce's head with the floor hockey stick, but quickly dismissed the idea. Even for me, that would be a definite overreaction to a *clarence*. Besides, the Kobels would only team up and pummel me into paste after school.

So I pulled up my sweats, dropped my head, and charged across the gym like a raging defensive tackle. My plan was simple. I'd head-butt Pierce in his intestines and knock him over. That would discourage him from trying another *clarence* on me.

Stupid move.

Pierce, like a skillful matador, stepped out of the way. And that allowed me a clear run at Mr. Woloski, who was walking over to see what the problem was.

Thadump!

My head torpedoed the gym teacher's stomach.

"Ow!" I yelled.

"Oooh," Mr. Woloski moaned.

"I'm sorry, sir," I apologized. "It was an accident. I didn't mean to blast my head into your gut."

Mr. Woloski was bent over, making a funny, panting noise. His face was pomegranate red and his eyes were all bulgey.

I noticed my best friend, Jonathan Stewart, giving me a sympathetic look.

"I was trying to peg Pierce," I went on. "Did you

see what he did to me? He pulled a *clarence*. If it makes you feel any better, sir, my head hurts a lot."

"Enough," Mr. Woloski wheezed. He straightened up and sucked a couple of deep breaths. "I . . . will . . . not . . . put . . . up . . . with . . . this . . .," he puffed as his breathing slowly returned to normal.

"I'm truly, honestly sorry," I said again.

"Sorry is not good enough." His voice got stronger and angrier with each word. "You just bought yourself a visit to the DT Dungeon, Stormalong."

"That's not fair, Mr. Woloski. It was an accident. How come I'm being punished for something Pierce did? It wouldn't have happened if Pierce hadn't pulled a *clarence* on me."

"Do you want two days?" he snapped.

I noticed Jonathan fanning his face with his hand. That was his way of telling me to cool it.

So what else is new, I thought. It's just another normal day in the life of Stormalong Sprague.

Little did I know how destiny was working.

Mr. Woloski recovered from my skull plant to his abdomen and made the class sit in a half circle on the gym floor.

"Before you get changed, I have a very important announcement," he began. "On Friday, we'll begin the floor hockey tournament for the Mallory Trophy."

I picked at my fingernails, only half listening. I was growing them long on my left hand, so I'd be able to play my electric guitar when my folks bought me one for Christmas. If I learned to play heavy metal, maybe people would stop teasing me.

"As you know," Mr. Woloski droned on, "the

teams must be mixed. They may consist of three boys and two girls or vice versa."

This was the third time we'd heard the speech. The gym teacher had been psyching us up for the tournament since Thanksgiving.

"Just to refresh your memory," Mr. Woloski continued, "Morton Mallory is an ex-student of Taft Junior High. Burlington, Vermont, is his hometown. He had physical education classes in this very gym. He may have sat exactly where you're sitting. Of course, I don't have to detail the outstanding career Mr. Mallory had with the New York Rangers of the National Hockey League in the nineteen eighties."

Jock strap hero worship, I thought.

"For the last five years the seventh graders have competed in a floor hockey competition in Mr. Mallory's honor. The teams must have two forwards, two defence, and a goalie. The tournament will be played in the large gym using the school's plastic hockey sticks and a plastic puck. The winning team will have their names engraved on the Mallory Trophy."

"A goal worth dying for," I whispered to Jonathan.

"I want each of you to think seriously about forming a team with the girls."

"Yo, yo, yo!" Pierce and Adon hooted and pounded on the floor with their fists. "Floor hockey! Girls! Floor hockey! Yo, yo, yo!"

Mr. Woloski looked proudly at the twins and then at the whole seventh grade class. "That's the famous Taft spirit, boys," he said.

When he glanced at me, I tried not to look completely bored out of my gourd.

* * *

Jonathan and I sat in the cafeteria, the only people at our table.

"I don't deserve a detention," I complained. "It was an accident."

"Whatever you say." Jonathan peeled a banana and studied its bruises. "You know, I hate bashed bananas. They taste different."

"Don't try to change the subject. You saw what happened. I don't deserve to get dumped in the Dungeon."

I noticed Pierce Kobel sitting at another table with Tulip Nixon, another seventh grader who can be nasty when she puts her mind to it. They were looking at me and laughing. No doubt, Pierce was detailing my misadventure in fine detail. I made a mental note to delete Tulip from my Girls-I-want-to-spend-a-vacation-in-Hawaii-with-when-I-get-rich-and-famous list.

"A true friend would stick up for me," I insisted.

"I'm the best friend you've got," he said.

I couldn't argue with that. Jonathan is my only friend. We don't do all that much together. We're more or less friends by default. We became friends in the sixth grade because nobody else liked us.

People bug me because I do and say stupid things. Jonathan gets razzed because his favorite activity in the whole world is dancing. He dances with his cousin Elaine. They do ballroom stuff: the waltz, tango, rumba, things like that. He spends most weekends competing in different dance contests.

He's good at it, has a wall of trophies, and lots of fancy dance suits. But the belief among the boys at Taft Junior High is that *real guys don't dance*. They think ballroom dancing is a sissy thing to do.

5

Because Jonathan insisted, I once tried his dance classes for a couple of weeks. I got frustrated trying to get my feet to do things they obviously didn't want to do. I thought it would be easy, but it was worse than gym class—too much sweaty work. So I quit.

If people understood how tough dancing is, I'm sure they'd have a different attitude toward Jonathan. There's nothing sissy about it at all.

I continued to complain. "Pierce pulled a *clarence* on me."

"I wonder where it got that name?" Jonathan asked. "Long ago, there was probably some boy in Taft Junior High named Clarence. Maybe pulling down his pants was how everyone teased him. Maybe even our wonderful hockey superstar, Morton Mallory, used to pull poor Clarence's sweatpants down."

"Morton Mallory," I scoffed. "Just because he played hockey for a few years, what's the big deal? The Mallory Trophy tournament is a waste of time."

"No it isn't," Jonathan disagreed. "I sort of like floor hockey. I wouldn't mind playing on a team."

That surprised me. "You would?"

He nodded. "Sure. But it won't happen. Nobody would ever ask me to be on their team."

"Okay, gentlemen, time to pay up," a voice interrupted us. It belonged to Dabny Paulty, a member of the Terminators, the closest thing Taft has to a gang.

The Terminators have shiny red jackets and hang around the Food Fair at the mall. Everyone in the gang has short hair with a small *T* razored on their left temple. For some reason I haven't been able to figure, they seem to impress all the good-looking girls.

Dabny's in our homeroom. He's a big guy with lots of muscles who is a year older than the rest of us. Rumor has it, he had to repeat first grade because he couldn't learn the alphabet. Also, Dabny's the only seventh grader in the Terminators. He's special because his older brother, Kevin the Barbarian, a ninth grader, is the gang leader.

"Time to pay up," Dabny repeated. "Let's see that silver George Washington."

I reached into my jeans pockets and tossed a quarter into Dabny's outstretched hand.

We paid the Terminators twenty-five cents a day for protection. This was supposed to insure that no evil came our way. What it insured was that the *Terminators* stayed out of our hair. They didn't care what other people like Pierce Kobel did.

"Where's yours, Stewart?" Dabny asked.

"I don't have any money," Jonathan replied.

"Run that by me again."

"I don't have any money," Jonathan repeated.

Dabny rubbed his chin and studied my friend for a few moments. "Okay, it's cool. I mean, this is the first time you've forgot. Just make sure you have fifty cents tomorrow." Then he broke into a broad grin. "Enjoy your lunch, gentlemen."

"You have money," I said when Dabny moved on. "You got change from lunch."

"I don't have any more money for the Terminators," Jonathan explained. "I've been thinking about it for a couple of weeks. Thinking that I'm going to stop paying them. Why should I give them twenty-five cents every day?"

"It's only a quarter," I pointed out. "It's nothing."

"It's the principle of it," Jonathan reasoned. "It's

7

against the Constitution or something. This isn't elementary school. What do you think is going to happen to us if we don't pay?"

"It's worth a quarter a day not to find out."

"The Terminators are all jerks," he declared.

I glanced around the room to make sure nobody had heard him. Then I added, "Course they are, but wouldn't you give your arm to be a member?"

He shook his head. "No way. Maybe a finger or two, but not a whole arm."

We both laughed.

Suddenly, Melvin Hardtack was looming over us. Melvin is the only seventh grader bigger than Dabny Paulty. And none of it is paunch. He glanced at my last cookie on the table. "Could I have that if you're not going to eat it?"

"Be my guest," I answered.

Melvin nodded a *thank you,* grabbed the cookie, and scarfed it in one swallow. "You got anything you're not going to finish, Jonathan?"

"Just some carrot sticks."

"I don't eat vegetables," Melvin informed us. "Thanks anyway." He went to the next table looking for more leftovers.

"I've noticed that Melvin doesn't give the Terminators a quarter," Jonathan said.

I didn't bother to comment on the obvious. Nobody was foolish enough to offer *protection* to Melvin Hardtack.

"He's been different lately," I said.

"Who?"

"Melvin, he's been more ... more human. I haven't seen him mad in weeks. Maybe months. He was always losing his temper in sixth grade. Remember?"

"Just don't refuse him when he wants a part of your lunch," Jonathan warned.

We laughed at that too.

"Did you see what Loreeta Simpson was wearing today?" I asked.

"No, but I noticed what Amber was wearing," he said. "She looks so good in that green sweater. Tonight, I'm going to phone her and ask if she wants to go to a movie with me on Friday."

"You can't be serious. There's no way Amber will go anywhere with you."

Jonathan bristled. "Why not?"

"Because you're in seventh grade."

"What's that got to do with anything? She's in seventh grade."

"Have you ever seen her do stuff with the rest of us? Dances? Watch a football game? Join any clubs?"

"No," he agreed. "In fact, I've never seen her with anybody in the school. In any grade. And I figure that probably means that she doesn't have a boyfriend."

"It just means that her boyfriends are in high school," I finished. "There's no way she'll go to a movie with you."

He winked at me. "We'll see."

Who would have thought how things were falling into place?

2.

The DT Dungeon

The DT Dungeon is the name somebody long ago gave to the detention room.

It fits.

The DT Dungeon is a utility room, half the size of a classroom, sandwiched between the industrial arts and boiler rooms on the first floor of Taft Junior High. The furniture consists of fifteen desks so old they're made of wood, and a metal teacher's desk so big it looks like it would take a crane to lift it.

There's nothing on the bulletin boards except for a poster of a cat hanging from a bar. The caption on it reads, *Hang in there, baby*. Somebody had drawn a beard on the cat. There's an old fire exit warning stapled on the wall next to the door. It says we should exit through a door they bricked up five years ago when they built the new gym.

The windows are covered with a gray film you can't scrape off. It makes the world appear permanently foggy. I wondered if the school hired a psychologist to decorate the DT Dungeon, to make sure whoever was inside would feel truly depressed. All it needed was an iron maiden and a rack.

I walked in and sat in my favorite spot in the front, so I could stare out the doorway, and checked out my fellow inmates in the Dungeon. There were five people in DT, and we were all seventh graders.

"Hurry up, Mr. Sprague. Look busy." Mr. Waddell sported his mean look.

I smiled at him. "Sure thing, sir. I'm just thinking what I should do."

"Do it fast," he threatened.

Mr. Waddell is the special supervisor at Taft. He's not a teacher—more or less a prison guard for junior high students. In one way, I feel sorry for him because special supervisor is a tough job. It has to rate with cleaning the toilets on a Klingon battlecruiser. He patrols the halls when we're in class. He watches the cafeteria at lunchtime. And he supervises the detention room from three until three-thirty. His job description must read, *Time people in the bathroom. Stop food fights. Tell DT kids to "Get busy."* It seems a depressing way to spend your middle age.

But in another way, I don't feel sorry for him at all. Mr. Waddell isn't exactly Mr. Personality. A lot of the time he's rude and sarcastic, like he's got a chip on one shoulder and an attitude on the other. He seems to enjoy belittling people.

"Mr. Sprague, you know the rules of the detention room." Mr. Waddell spoke real slow, like he was giving instructions to a first grader. "You are to do your homework or you are to read a book. Even you should be able to understand that."

"That's rude, sir," I pointed out.

Stupid thing to say.

Mr. Waddell fumed for a few moments. "I hope you enjoyed your outburst, Mr. Sprague, because it has earned you another day in here." He wrote something in his book.

"It wasn't an outburst, sir," I said as politely as possible. "It was just a comment."

"Are you looking for a visit to the principal's office?"

I shook my head.

"Then get out your homework or a library book," he repeated.

Just then, out of the corner of my eye, I saw someone walking past the open door. It was Loreeta Simpson, dressed in a pink sweatshirt and blue jeans, her purple hair bouncing over her shoulders. She glanced into the DT Dungeon, saw me, and broke into a wide and glorious grin.

Loreeta had transferred to Taft a couple of weeks ago from Burlington, Ontario, Canada. I thought it was an unusual coincidence for her to change countries and live in a city with the same name. The first time I saw her walk into homeroom, I thought, *There's the most beautiful girl in the whole world.*

She's not gorgeous in a Barbie-doll way. Or like the girls in music videos. She's more *interesting* than that. She has long hair, almost to her waist. It's a purpley color that changes shades from day to day. My mom told me that's because Loreeta uses a temporary rinse.

"Purple?" Mom had puzzled. "You like a girl with purple hair? Figures."

Loreeta's face reminds me of the zombie on my *Night of the Living Dead* poster I have pinned above my bed, only without the scars and the red eyes. The thing I like most about her is she has a big mouth. I mean that in a nice way. When she smiles she shows lots of teeth. Her face shines with enamel.

I smiled back at her, but she'd already walked by.

I have to talk to Loreeta before somebody tells her I'm a loser, I said to myself. I have to speak to her soon while she still thinks I'm normal.

"Get busy immediately," Mr. Waddell ordered.

I started to draw pictures of aliens on my math notes and thought about Loreeta Simpson. I was just completing an awesome slime worm with razor teeth and long feelers when Mr. Waddell stood up and stretched. "I have something important to do for a few minutes," he announced.

Translate that as, *I'm going to the bathroom to sneak a cigarette.*

"I don't want any talking in here while I'm out of the room," he went on.

Translate that as, *I know you're going to goof off; make sure you look innocent when I return.*

As soon as Mr. Waddell left, Joey Floozeman leaned over and tapped my shoulder. "You got any gum, Stormy?" he asked.

"Sorry, Joey," I answered. "What did you get a DT for?"

Joey drummed his fingers on his desk. "Waddell caught me running in the halls. I had to go to the bathroom. Real bad. It was an emergency."

"You should have told him."

"I did." Joey nodded and took a quick bite of a fingernail. "Mr. Waddell told me boys my age shouldn't have emergencies anymore."

"Then you should have told him you were running because that's the way you are."

All through elementary school, Joey was your classic hyper kid. He couldn't sit still at his desk for five minutes without falling onto the floor. I remember

13

him taking pills that were supposed to settle him down. They never seemed to make much difference.

"I've got some gum," a voice called from the back of the Dungeon. We turned around and watched Amber Littlewood put down her science textbook and search her purse. After a few seconds she pulled out a piece of Juicy Fruit and tossed it to Joey.

"Thanks," Joey said as he fumbled with the wrapper.

I continued to watch Amber. I could understand why Jonathan liked her. She was movie star–type beautiful. And she was severely devastating that day. Her blond hair waved over her shoulders, and her blue eyes sparkled like she had little Christmas tree lights behind her pupils. And what was under her green mohair sweater did justice to the fuzzy wool. But even with everything going for her, I didn't think Amber was as *interesting* as Loreeta Simpson.

"How come you have a DT, Amber?" Joey wanted to know.

"Ms. Pundit," she grumbled. "I'm three weeks behind on my science assignments. She sent me to the Dungeon so I can catch up."

Like I pointed out to Jonathan, I'd never seen Amber at a house league game or a sock hop. She just didn't do the things the rest of us did. I assumed she had more grown-up things to do, such as driving in hot cars and going to night clubs with guys.

"Want some gum, Stormy?" Joey asked.

"No, thanks. Chewing gum gives me a sore throat."

He turned to the girl sitting next to him and ripped the stick of gum in half. "How about you, Dimps?"

Dimps took the offering, making huge dimples appear on her cheeks. "Tank yu, Jokee."

Dimps came to the States from some place in Asia last summer. Her country used to be part of the USSR until the republics went their own ways. I forget what it's called. It's the one the newspeople on radio and TV have trouble saying.

And her name is just as hard to say, so nobody ever uses it. Everyone, including the teachers, calls her Dimps because her face turns into a mass of dimples when she smiles.

Dimps was trying to learn English, but was having a hard time with it. Half the day she stayed in the special needs room filling in first grade workbooks. She's not a DT person. After school, Mr. Waddell supervises her while she does extra work.

I checked out the book on Dimps's desk. I could tell it was some kind of math text, but I didn't have a clue what it was about. The questions were half numbers and half funny symbols. Dimps might be having a hard time with English, but she was a few light years ahead of us when it came to math and science.

Joey pointed at the book. "What are you working on?"

"I peg my bardon."

"It's 'I beg your pardon,' " I told Dimps.

She nodded at me. "I peg yur bardon, Jokee."

Joey chomped on another fingernail. "The book. What's the book about?"

Dimps made another face full of tiny baby bottoms. "Ah, da buk." She lifted it off her desk. "Diz buk iz krap."

Amber and I laughed.

"Who told you it was crap?" I asked.

Dimps concentrated on my words for a few moments, then waved her book in the direction of the last occupant of the DT Dungeon. "Melkin say it krap."

That made Amber laugh louder.

Melvin Hardtack looked at Amber and smiled. It wasn't a big smile, more or less a glorified grimace, but it was still a smile. *Melvin smile?* I thought. I tried to remember the last time I'd seen him smile. Had I ever seen it? What could possibly make Melvin do something so odd? I quickly came to the conclusion there were only two possibilities. Either Melvin had gone insane or else hormones were happening.

It had to be hormones. Just like Jonathan, Melvin had the hots for Amber.

"Why are you in the Dungeon?" I asked Melvin.

"Mrs. Dawson said I was being rude," he grumbled.

"What were you doing?" Joey wondered.

"I wasn't doing nothing," he answered. "I was just looking at her."

"Your looks can be a little rude at times," I blurted.

Stupid thing to say.

Melvin's face creased into a road map of anger lines.

I frantically tried to think of a way to save my life. "What I mean is," I stuttered, "you have a really powerful face. Strong. Full of dignity."

But fate was working in its weird way. Joey Floozeman came to my rescue. "Hey, Stormy," he said, "you'll never guess the fantastic idea I got today."

3.

Wat Iz Fur Hooky?

"I was thinking about what Mr. Woloski said this morning," Joey began. "You know, about the Mallory Trophy and the floor hockey tournament. I think it would be a wonderful idea if I was the captain of a floor hockey team."

"That's a terrific idea, Joey," I said as I watched Melvin. To my surprise, Joey's interruption seemed to chill the big guy out. He'd closed his eyes and appeared to be concentrating on his breathing. Most strange. And most fortunate for me. I still had a skull in one piece.

"Do you want to be on my team, Stormy?" Joey asked. "Do you want to play for the Mallory Trophy?"

"Huh?"

"Do you want to play on my hockey team?"

Joey had to be pulling my leg. "You're kidding?"

He fidgeted in his desk. "We'll have fun."

"Me and you and floor hockey?"

He bobbed his head.

"You can't be serious."

He bobbed his head again.

"Don't be a turkey, Joey."

"Come on, Stormy," he coaxed. "Don't you want your name engraved on the Mallory Trophy? Don't you

17

want people a thousand years from now to see your name carved on that piece of silver?"

"It's aluminum," I pointed out. "And the answer is *no*."

"Think of the glory."

"Give me a break."

"Think of the rest of the team, then," Joey coached. "The team needs you."

"The team?" I wondered how Joey found anybody in seventh grade who wanted to be on his team. "Who else is playing?"

"There isn't a whole bunch of people," he confessed.

"Who then?"

"Just me. So far. But I'm going to get others. Like Dimps."

"Dimps?"

He nodded. "Sure. Hey, Dimps, you want to play on my floor hockey team?"

"I peg yur bardon, Jokee."

"You want to play floor hockey?"

"Wat iz fur hooky?"

"Just say *yes*," Joey insisted.

"Kes." Dimps did as she was told.

Joey grinned at me. "See. Now there's three of us."

I laughed. "Get real. This is so dumb. I don't believe—"

Joey didn't let me finish. He whipped around so he was facing Amber. "How about you, Amber? You want to be on my floor hockey team?"

She rubbed her forehead. "Don't bug me, please. I need to concentrate on this science."

"Please, Amber," Joey pleaded. "Stormy, Dimps, and me need you."

"Wait a minute," I interjected. "Who said I was on your team?"

"I'm really not interested," Amber affirmed.

Joey continued to plead. "I'll let you be the goalie."

"Please leave me alone." She shook her head slowly and muttered something under her breath.

"What if I do you a big, big favor?" Joey tried a bribe. "What if I do your science project for you? Would you play on my team then?"

She stiffened in her seat, giving Joey her full attention. "My science project?"

"You're having trouble with science. You said you were in the Dungeon because you're three weeks behind. The term project is due next week. It's worth fifty percent of the report card mark. You started it yet?"

Amber hesitated. "Kind of."

"Oh yeah?" Joey said. "What's your topic?"

"Fish," Amber told him. "I guess I'll do a project on fish."

"Fish!?" Joey chuckled. "We're studying plants this term, not animals."

"I know that," Amber defended.

"Then you must also know the project has to be on plants," Joey said. "Look, Amber, what if I make you a great display on photosynthesis? Would you play on my team then?"

"You'd do that for me?" Amber asked. "You'd do my project?"

"Sure," Floozeman agreed. "All you have to do is be our goalie."

"I heard you!" Mr. Waddell pointed a stubby finger at Joey as he strode into the class. "I said *no talking*. What's so important, Mr. Floozeman? You'd better have a good explanation or else you'll be sitting here tomorrow afternoon."

"I was just asking Amber if she wanted to be on my floor hockey team," Joey explained.

Mr. Waddell sat at his desk and wiggled a finger in his ear to indicate he didn't believe what he'd just heard. *"You* have a floor hockey team, Mr. Floozeman?"

Joey's grin stretched across his face. "You bet. Stormy is on it."

Mr. Waddell's laughter thundered off the bare walls of the DT Dungeon. "Thank you. Thank you," the special supervisor chuckled. "You have made my day, Mr. Floozeman. You and Mr. Sprague on a floor hockey team? Just the thought of it is so incredibly . . . humorous. Talk about a team of dregs."

"What do you mean by that?" I asked.

"Well, Mr. Sprague, you do know what the word *dreg* means, don't you?"

"Yeah," I answered. "It's the crud that's left over after the good stuff is gone."

"Precisely," Mr. Waddell said. "It's the leftovers in the bottom of a pickle jar after the pickles are gone. And in a way, it describes you and Mr. Floozeman, doesn't it?"

"I don't want to be rude," I shot back. "But you're being rude."

Mr. Waddell didn't dump on me. Instead, he flashed a smug grin. "I am merely stating a fact, Mr. Sprague. The boys and girls who end up in the DT Dungeon are obviously what's left over after the *good stuff* is gone. In this case, after the normal students have gone home."

If Mr. Waddell was a teacher, he wouldn't be allowed to say that. Even a special supervisor shouldn't be allowed to insult us.

"It would be so funny to see you two running around the gymnasium making complete fools out of yourselves," Mr. Waddell continued. "It's too bad you don't really have a team."

"We do," Joey said. "That's why I was asking Amber to join."

Mr. Waddell studied Amber for a moment. "You would certainly fit, Miss Littlewood. I would be most amused to see *you* trying to play floor hockey."

I watched Amber's face turn a neat shade of burgundy. For a moment I thought she'd lost it and was going to say something that would be worth a suspension. But her words came out strong and determined. "I hope you enjoy watching, Mr. Waddell, because I plan to be the goalie." Then she turned to Joey. "I accept your offer."

Joey clapped his hands together. "Great, that means we only need one more person."

"You got him," Melvin called. "Count me in."

I stared at Melvin in disbelief.

"Wow!" Even Joey was amazed. "With Melvin on our side, we're a contender."

Mr. Waddell seemed to share our amazement. "The dregs of the DT Dungeon have a team? Nobody is going to believe this in the faculty lounge tomorrow morning."

At three-thirty Amber, Dimps, Melvin, Joey, and I left the Dungeon in a bunch. As soon as we got in the hall, I turned around and held out my arms to stop everyone.

"Now let me get this straight," I said. "I have this spooky feeling I'm in the middle of a *Twilight Zone* rerun. I just had a weird dream where you guys agreed to be a team in the Mallory Trophy floor hockey thing. I want you to tell me it was only my imagination."

"It's not just us." Joey beamed. "It's you too. You're on the team."

I scratched my head. "That's just it. I don't recall volunteering."

"You don't want to play?" Melvin snarled. "What's wrong with us? You think you're better than the rest of us, Sprague?"

"Course not. And I'd rather be on your team than against your team."

"Good," Melvin said. "Because I hate snobby people."

"Me? A snob? I'm a lot of things, but snob isn't one of them. All I'm saying is I'm having a hard time picturing us as a floor hockey team. You don't play house league sports, Mel. Why would you want to be on a floor hockey team now?"

"I got my reasons," Melvin declared. His eyes flicked to where Amber and Dimps were standing. Hormones again.

"And what about you, Amber?" I went on. "You're like Melvin. You never play house league. Heck, you never do anything with us outside of class."

"Joey's doing my project," she pointed out. "It's worth standing in goal for a few minutes for that."

"A few minutes is a half hour," I said. "And the

other team will be drilling a little plastic puck at incredible speeds to the bruisable parts of your body."

Her expression changed to a worried look. "I didn't think of that."

"Don't worry about it, Amber," Joey said. "It'll be fun. We can win. We can be the floor hockey champs."

"Wat iz fur hooky?" Dimps wondered.

4.

Amber and Loreeta

On my way home, I stopped at Jonathan's house. His dad answered the door.

"Hello, Stormy. How's school?" Mr. Stewart asks me the same question every time he sees me.

"Fine." I always answer the same way. "Is Jonathan home?"

"Yes, but I don't think you have much time to visit. He has to go to his dance lesson in a few minutes."

"I'll only be a little while," I said as I flipped off my runners.

Mr. Stewart has a thing about wearing street shoes in the house. He makes Jonathan wear slippers. "Sometimes I feel like I'm a character in a Norman Rockwell painting," Jonathan once said when I teased him about his in-house footwear.

"Don't be long, Stormy," Mr. Stewart ordered. "Jonathan and I are leaving as soon as I finish my sandwich."

I swallowed the comment that wanted to roll out of my lips about how it wasn't suppertime and maybe Mr. Stewart should skip the sandwich because he already had a weight problem. Mr. Stewart has never been the same to me since the day I asked him, "Have you always been fat?"

24

A stupid thing to say.

I climbed the stairs, tapped on Jonathan's bedroom door, and entered when I heard, "Come on in." Jonathan was standing in front of his mirror admiring himself. "Hi, partner," he said.

"New costume?" I asked.

"I told you, they're not called costumes. They're suits. Girls wear costumes. Guys wear suits. And, yes, it's new. You like it?"

"Yeah, sort of Mexican. But the slippers look a little dumb."

"It's Spanish, not Mexican," he corrected. "Enough with the slipper jokes. I'll be wearing boots. With Cuban heels. I'm going to wear this outfit when Elaine and I go to the tango competition in Montreal next month."

"It looks great. But the pants are real tight," I pointed out. "Don't they hurt? It must be hard to bend over in those without it hurting. I once had a tight pair of jeans which almost crippled me. Know what I mean?"

"It doesn't hurt. The material stretches."

"Can I borrow them? I bet if I was wearing those pants, I'd really be able to impress Loreeta Simpson."

He smiled. "You serious?"

I shook my head. "No, I'm kidding. But I'd really like to impress Loreeta. She flashed me a smile in the Dungeon this afternoon."

"Loreeta had a detention?"

"No, she just walked by the door. You had to see the smile on her face, Jonathan. It was so . . . wide."

"If you like her so much, why don't you go up and talk to her?"

"I've been thinking how," I told him. "I need

something to talk about. I'm afraid I'll say or do something stupid. You know what I'm like."

"So call her on the phone then," he suggested. "That's easy."

"I don't know her number. She just moved, so it won't be in the book."

"Call information," Jonathan said. "Ask for a new listing for Simpson."

"Good idea. I'll do that right after supper. That'll give me enough time to think of something to talk about."

"Speaking of calling a girl," Jonathan said as he sat on his bed and picked up the extension phone on the night table. "This is a good time to call Amber." He punched in a number. "Five, five, five, one, two, one, three, home of the Littlewoods."

"Right." I laughed. "You can't fool me. You just called the weather or Dial-a-Prayer or something."

"Hello," Jonathan said. "Is that Amber?"

Pause.

"Yeah, hi, it's Jonathan."

Pause.

"Right, Jonathan Stewart, the guy with the curly hair."

Pause.

"I never really thought about it. I guess I am sort of cute."

I continued to laugh. "Very funny, but stop it. I have something to tell you before you go out."

"Well, I was wondering," Jonathan went on, "if you're not doing anything on Friday night, maybe you'd like to go see the new Kevin Costner movie at the mall."

"Knock it off," I said. "I know you're not talking to Amber."

"Of course I'm serious," Jonathan said to the phone.

"Hang up and stop being a bozo."

"Oh, okay," Jonathan's voice dropped a few decibels. "Sure, I understand."

Pause.

"All right. Yeah, I'll see you at school. 'Bye." Then Jonathan thrust the receiver in my direction.

Loud and clear, I heard Amber Littlewood say, "Good-bye."

He hung up.

"Wow!" I gasped. "That was really her. You called Amber."

"She can't go out Friday. She's baby-sitting."

"You called Amber." I was still in a state of shock. "Most impressive! When did you get so brave?"

"Jonathan," his father called.

"I've got to go, Stormy."

"Wait. I have to tell you this. You'll never guess what happened in the Dungeon today. . . ."

I quickly explained how Joey had formed a floor hockey team. When I was finished, Jonathan stared at me like I'd suddenly turned into an alien.

"Close your mouth and stop looking like that," I said.

"I'm sorry." He shook the stunned look off his face. "It's just that I can't believe you're on a floor hockey team."

"I'm not," I said. "Then again, maybe I am. I didn't say I would. But I didn't say I wouldn't either."

"It's so hard to believe," Jonathan observed. "Amber playing floor hockey. I can't picture it."

"She's trying to pass science," I explained.

"What?"

"Let's go, Son," Mr. Stewart called again.

"I'll tell you later," I said.

"Joey? Melvin? Dimps?" Jonathan mused as he grabbed a sweater from his closet. "What a team."

"So you think I should join?"

"Course I do. If you don't, tell Joey I'd love to be on his team. I'm jealous you're going to play hockey with my future girlfriend."

I followed him down the stairs. "You going to go out with Dimps?"

"Someday Amber will see what a wonderful person I am," he declared. "Sooner than you think."

I picked up my little brother Brandon from Mrs. Kellock, our next-door neighbor. Brandon is in second grade, and Mrs. Kellock baby-sits him after school until I get home. She likes having him over because she has a toddler, Jessica, and Brandon plays with the little kid.

My folks work in the auto parts factory. When they're on afternoon shifts, Brandon is my responsibility. I don't mind the chore at all. It leaves me free to work on him. One of my missions in life is to make sure Brandon grows up half normal, so he doesn't get picked on like me.

"What did you learn in school today?" I asked when we got home.

"Nothing."

"Come on. You must have learned something."

"Nothing. What's for supper?"

I poked around in the fridge. "Let's see. Um, looks good tonight. Mom's left Shake 'n Bake for small rodents. All we have to do is catch a couple of mice and it'll go great with the mashed leech soup Dad made last night."

Brandon giggled.

"So is Darry still giving you a hard time?" I wanted to know.

Darry Paulty is the younger incarnation of Dabny and Kevin. He's doing his best to follow in his brothers' footsteps. Several times he's tried to tease Brandon into a fight. Fortunately for my sibling, a teacher showed up at the right time. But I knew from experience that Brandon's luck wouldn't hold out forever.

"Darry wasn't at school today," Brandon answered as I handed him the tuna casserole from the fridge. He popped it into the microwave and keyed the controls to High.

"I'm still thinking how you can handle the little snot," I said. "I'll come up with a plan."

We sat at the kitchen table, waiting for the casserole to bubble.

"Did you ever get picked on in second grade, Stormy?"

"All the time. I told you, I've been picked on every day of my life. Sometimes I think I've been put on earth so other people can give me a hard time."

"Then I'll just do what you did?" Brandon reasoned.

"You haven't been listening to me," I lectured. "You never, ever do what I did. Everything I did in elementary school was wrong. That's why I'm having a hard time in junior high. My reputation is following me around."

"I like your funny stories."

"They might sound funny, but they're not. They're pathetic."

Brandon disagreed. "I think it's funny you ate the dead fish from the class aquarium in kindergarten."

"I thought it would impress everyone," I explained. "I thought chomping on the guppy we found floating in the tank would make people like me. The only thing it did was make me puke on the paint table. Everyone pegged me as a geek."

"It was funny when you drove your bike through the principal's window."

"That was in third grade. And my bike didn't go through the window, just me. I was lucky the window was open. I was goofing around and didn't see the wall."

Brandon started to laugh. "I can just see the look on Mrs. Klassen's face when you landed on her desk."

I chuckled too. "She was slightly surprised."

"And it was funny when the ambulance guys took you away last year."

I grimaced. "Don't remind me."

Definitely one of my most embarrassing moments. A kid called Mark Butcher was looking to destroy me because I'd accidentally bumped into his table at McDonald's. I'd offered to buy him a new lunch, but he was upset about the milkshake soaking into his crotch. He'd counteroffered with a plan to remove my head from my neck. I'd said *no thanks* and charged out of the restaurant.

I knew it was just a matter of time until Mark

made good on his threat, so I worked out what I thought was an ingenious plan.

"I knew Mark was going to find me," I told Brandon. "But I figured I could scare him off if he thought I had rabies."

"So you put some baking soda in a sandwich bag," Brandon said.

"Right. And I carried it around in my pocket. When I saw Mark walking down the street, I popped the baking soda into my mouth. It started fizzing and foaming, drooling out of my mouth. I jumped up and down and yelled about how I wasn't feeling so good ever since I got bitten by a crazy skunk."

"Great stuff," Brandon praised.

"It worked. Mark took one look at me and started running down the street. He never bothered me again. Would you want to mess with somebody flopping around with white foam oozing out his mouth?"

"Great stuff."

"Then the off-duty ambulance drove by. What was the chance of that? And what was the chance the attendants would stop and take me to the hospital because they thought I was having a convulsion?"

"A what?"

"A fit. It was a stupid thing to do."

Brandon couldn't stop laughing. He fell off the chair, grabbed his gut, and began rocking on the floor.

"And it helped label me as even more strange," I concluded. "Don't ever do what I did, Bran. I don't want you to end up like me."

With Brandon watching a *Star Trek: The Next Generation* rerun and the supper dishes in the dishwasher, I picked up the phone and dialled 411. The operator gave me the new listing for Simpson, and I quickly punched the numbers before I lost my courage. A woman answered. I asked for Loreeta and she politely told me to wait. A few moments later, Loreeta picked up the phone.

"Hello," she said.

Stupid me! I'd called her and I didn't have a clue what I was going to talk about.

"Hello?"

"Hi."

"Yes? Who is this?"

"Hi."

"Who is this?"

"Hi."

"Is this some kind of joke?" she asked.

"Hi."

Jeez, I had to say something. I couldn't let her think I was some kind of weirdo. "I just wanted to welcome you to Burlington."

So far so good, I thought.

"Thank you. Who is this?"

"My name's Stormalong Sprague. Everybody calls me Stormy. I'm in your homeroom."

"Oh, yes." Loreeta actually sounded pleased it was me. "You sit next to me in math."

She'd noticed.

"I saw you walking by when I was in the Dungeon this afternoon. You have a nice smile."

"Thank you."

"You have a lot of teeth."

Stupid thing to say.

"Thanks . . . I guess."

I tried to recover. "Your teeth really suit you."

Another stupid thing to say.

"I'm sorry, Loreeta," I apologized. "What I'm saying is coming out all wrong. What I mean to say is that I think you're really pretty."

"Thank you." The delight returned to her voice. I could picture her sitting in her house, all those teeth gleaming.

"Why were you in DT?" she asked.

"Because Pierce Kobel pulled a *clarence* on me in gym class."

"A *clarence*? What's that?"

I felt suddenly embarrassed. I couldn't explain to her that Pierce had yanked down my sweats so that I was standing around in my jockeys. I couldn't say "underwear" to Loreeta Simpson. Besides, if I told her the truth she might put two and two together. Only the dweebos end up being *clarenced*.

"What's a *clarence?*" she asked again.

"I have to go now."

"Why? You just called. Is something wrong?" She sounded disappointed.

"Er . . . er . . . my cat is on fire."

"Your cat is on fire?"

"It's just a little one. It's just its head," I said as I hung up the receiver. Then I pounded my temple with my fist. You moron. The cat's head is on fire? What part of your stupid brain did that come from?

Stupid, stupid thing to say.

What did Loreeta Simpson think of me now?

5.

The Dregs

That night, I lay in bed thinking, Do I really want to be on Joey's team? Do I really want to play hockey for the Mallory Trophy?

Playing floor hockey wasn't something Stormalong Sprague did. It was too normal. Yet, when I was honest with myself, that was the reason the idea appealed to me. Being in the competition was such a *regular* thing to do. If I played, maybe everyone would think, Stormy is one of us after all. Maybe Loreeta would think, He's normal, even if his cat's head is on fire.

I worried if there was a chance that by playing on this particular team, I'd end up looking even weirder. I mean, Hyperman Joey Floozeman as my captain? Melvin Hardtack as my teammate? Their reputations were only slightly less strange than mine. And Amber? Most bizarre.

Then again, being on the same team with such different people, all doing a normal thing, could only make us seem like everybody else. Besides, there was Dimps. Everybody liked her, even though we couldn't say her name and didn't understand most of what she said.

I knew we'd never win the Mallory Trophy, but we had Melvin going for us. And Joey wasn't a bad player. I was completely useless in almost everything in gym. Except floor hockey. I knew I could play mediocre-okay, if I wanted to. And maybe Dimps would turn out to be a natural. Maybe she was a floor hockey star in wherever she's from. Amber might surprise us too. She might make some incredible saves. Whatever, we were good enough so we wouldn't get laughed out of the gym.

All in all, I figured I didn't have anything to lose.

When I walked into homeroom the next morning, I noticed Loreeta smiling at me, showing all those perfectly formed incisors and bicuspids. What an incredible grin. She bounced out of her desk and skipped over to me. "Thanks for calling last night."

I waited for her to add, "You really are a dork, you know." But she didn't. She continued to smile. "You have a great sense of humor."

"What?" I puzzled.

"The comment about your cat's head being on fire was really funny."

"It was?"

"I couldn't stop laughing after you hung up." She began to chuckle. "It's still funny now."

"It is?"

"Of course. I've always admired people who have a sense of humor. I wish I could think up funny things like that. You must be proud of your talent."

"I guess so. . . ."

She reached over and brushed my shoulder. "There was a hair there," she explained. "I was wondering—have you started your science project yet?"

"Uh-uh. I'm still debating on a topic. I'll have to start tonight."

She twisted some purpley hair around a finger.

"Maybe you'd like to do your project with me? We're allowed to work with a partner."

It took me a half nanosecond to agree. "Great. When do you want to start? I could meet you in the library at lunch."

She thought for a moment. "The library is always so busy. I was thinking that we could work someplace more private. Maybe you'd like to come over to my house tonight."

"Huh?" I couldn't have heard that right.

She looked disappointed. "Course, if you don't want to . . ."

I closed my mouth and tried to act casual. First, I had to confirm what I thought I'd heard. "Did you just invite me to your house?"

She nodded.

"Me and you? Alone? In your house? Working on a science project?"

She nodded again. "We wouldn't be completely alone. My mom would be there and my younger brother, Brett, will probably be around too. But we could work in my bedroom. They won't bother us."

I tried to make spit. Why was my mouth so dry? This had to be a joke. Somebody had set up Loreeta to do this. This was another *let's-play-a-funny-trick-on-Stormy* ruse.

I glanced around the classroom, studying faces, looking for that telltale smile on the face of someone teasing me. I didn't find it. Except for Joey Floozeman, nobody was looking at me. Joey was too nice to think up this kind of a trick.

Loreeta was regarding me, puzzled, no doubt wondering why I was acting like a dyslexic monkey.

"Okay," I said. I expected to hear a symphony of

laughter. I expected to hear, "Stormy's fallen for another one."

Nothing.

"Around seven would be fine," Loreeta told me.

I spent first period English class wondering what was going on. *I like your sense of humor. Come over to my house tonight.* It had to be some kind of practical joke. But as the morning wore on and nobody slapped me on the back and said, "Hey, we had you going, didn't we? You didn't really believe Loreeta would invite a pea brain like you to her house?", it dawned on me that what had happened had *really* happened. Loreeta Simpson, the most beautiful girl in the entire world, wanted to do her science project with me in her bedroom.

Anybody who wanted to enter a team in the Mallory Trophy Competition had to sign up in the gym office during lunch.

"I think all five of us should go," Joey said to me during morning break. "It's really important for us to mesh, to work on our team concept. We have to be in top form mentally, as well as physically."

"Do you realize how silly you sound?" I asked. "Just kidding," I added, when I saw the hurt look on his face.

It turned out the only person who went to register with Joey was me.

Melvin decided that eating an adequate lunch was more important. "I've got to hang around the lunchroom," he said. "I never know who's going to offer me their dessert."

Dimps obviously hadn't understood what Joey told her because she went to Ms. Bhullar's room to watch

Sesame Street on TV, which is another way she's supposed to be learning English.

And Amber had a previous engagement. To my surprise, she was going to the Burger King with Kevin Paulty.

"What are you and Kevin going to do at the Burger King?" Joey wanted to know.

"Eat lunch," Amber said.

"Is this a date?" Joey probed. "You going on a lunchtime date with Kevin?"

"Why would you think that, Joey?" Amber asked.

"I'm just curious," he told Amber. "I want to know what people do on a date. I might go on a date someday soon and I want to know what to do. We're teammates now. I help you with your science project. You teach me everything you know about dating."

"It's not a date," Amber insisted. "He's going to buy me lunch."

Joey winked at me as Amber turned and walked down the hall. "Lucky Kevin, huh?"

Amber and Kevin? I decided not to tell Jonathan.

The door to the gym office was open. Mr. Woloski was marking a pile of health tests. "Come in, boys," he said when he saw us.

"I'm here to enter my team in the floor hockey tournament," Joey announced.

"Amazing." Mr. Woloski seemed genuinely pleased to hear it, sort of happy and surprised at the same time.

"I'm the captain." Joey beamed.

"Amazing," the gym teacher repeated. Then he studied me. "And what do you want, Stormy? Are you here to tell me you've forgotten your gym strip again?"

"I'm on Joey's team, sir."

"Amazing." He was sure stuck on the same adjective. "I'm pleased to see you taking an interest in an athletic activity. You're not my most enthusiastic student, Stormy."

I figured that was teacher talk for saying, "You're an uncoordinated mass of protoplasm."

"Phys. ed. is tough for guys like me," I said.

"How so?" Mr. Woloski wanted to know.

"It's forty-five minutes a day of total humiliation," I declared. "First, we have to get undressed in front of each other. Maybe jocks like changing into their sweats as a group, but some of us find it embarrassing. Then you make us do those stupid drills. Do you know how embarrassing it is when you're the only person in class who can't serve a volleyball *over* the net? Or do a lay-up shot in basketball. And what about fitness testing? Do you know how much you get teased when you can only do three push-ups? Sometimes I think gym teachers get a big thrill watching people like me grunt and groan trying to touch our toes."

Do you really think you should have said that to your gym teacher? the little voice in my head said.

Mr. Woloski's eyebrows were knitted together. I quickly tried damage control. "Of course, I don't mean you, Mr. Woloski. You're not a gym teacher like that. You're a terrific gym teacher. . . ."

He frowned. "Perhaps you should stop while you're still ahead, Stormy."

"Yes, sir."

I noticed Mr. Woloski rub his stomach a couple of times. Maybe he was thinking about yesterday.

"Tell me who else is on your team, Joey," Mr. Woloski said.

"There's Dimps," Joey began. "I don't know her real name. She's the new girl. The one who can't speak English."

"Oh, yes." The gym teacher nodded. Obviously he didn't know Dimps's name either.

"Amber's on my team too," Joey went on.

Mr. Woloski bit the end of his pen. "That certainly is . . . amazing."

"Melvin is our last player," Joey said.

"Melvin Hardtack is on a floor hockey team?" Mr. Woloski gasped. "I find all this . . ."

"Amazing," I offered.

"Exactly the right word, Stormy," he agreed. "What do you call your team, boys?"

Joey looked at me. "Gee, I don't know," he said.

I shrugged my shoulders to tell him that I didn't have any suggestions.

"I guess because it was my idea, we could name the team after me," Joey went on. "How about we call us Floozeman's Floozies. What do you think, Stormy?"

"I think that's dumb, Joey. Amber definitely won't want to be called a Floozie."

"Why not?"

"Trust me."

Just then some other people arrived to register their team. Mr. Woloski instructed us to think about our name and get back to him. We shuffled out of the office and sat on the bottom bleachers in the large gym.

"I still think Floozies is a good name," Joey insisted.

"Look it up in the dictionary," I told him. "It doesn't fit our team."

"Okay, if you think so. What about the word Mr. Waddell called us in the Dungeon yesterday?" he suggested. "We can call ourselves the Dregs."

"That was an insult," I pointed out.

"Not really," Joey reasoned. "It means we're different. Special. Everybody else will pick dumb names like Hawks, Tigers, Chiefs. We don't want a stupid name like that, do we?"

"I don't know," I balked. "Are we the stuff left over?"

"A lot of the other kids think we are," Joey said. "Let's show them what we can do."

"I don't—"

"It's either the Dregs or the Floozies. What's your choice?"

I didn't say anything.

"The Dregs it is," Joey said. "I'll go tell Mr. Woloski."

As I walked down the hall toward the cafeteria, I noticed Dabny Paulty coming the other way. He held out his arm, "I'm looking for that silver first president."

I dropped a quarter into his hand as I passed by. Then, to my surprise, he grabbed the back of my sweatshirt and twisted me around.

"Wait a minute, Sprague," he ordered. "Maybe I should talk to you about this problem I got. You and Jonathan Stewart are close buds, correct? You hang out together."

"So?"

"So tell your friend he's heading for trouble if he doesn't pay up."

"What?"

"Don't be so thick. He owes the Terminators twenty-five cents a day. He refused to pay me today. That's two days in a row."

"He did?"

"Tell him it isn't healthy," Dabny warned. "My brother Kevin won't be happy. Tell him it's worth two bits to have the Terminators looking out for you. You're smart enough to know that, huh?"

I nodded.

"Then tell your friend all sorts of things can happen to him," Dabny finished. "Make him understand."

I continued to nod. *What's got into Jonathan?* I thought.

6.

What's Wrong?

"I'm not going to pay anymore," Jonathan told me in the cafeteria. "It's stupid. What are they going to do to me?"

"Turn you into pizza sauce," I guessed. "Rip out your pancreas. Blow up your house. Put fleas in your jock strap. A million other things."

"That's crazy."

"No, it's not," I told him. "You are."

He bit a carrot stick, chomped on it for a while, and pointed what was left of the vegetable into my face. "I'm crazy? I'm not still paying them like somebody I know. What is his name? Stormy something?"

"It's only a dollar twenty-five a week," I said. "You can't even buy a comic book for a buck and a quarter."

"That has nothing to do with it. What they're doing is wrong. I'm not going to be part of it anymore."

I grimaced at the vision of what the Terminators might do. "Kevin the Barbarian will have to make an example of you. He'll have to eat your face so the rest of us don't stop paying."

"I don't believe that, Stormy."

"You can't afford to take the chance."

He finished the carrot, swallowed, and leaned back in the chair. "You have to stop being such a wimp."

"A wimp?" I thought for a moment. "Okay, maybe I am. But I *admit* it. I don't want the Terminators beating on my internal organs. But you're a wimp too. Why are you acting so brave all of a sudden. Everybody knows you dance."

Stupid thing to say.

"Pardon me?" Jonathan's face radiated disbelief and anger.

I buried my face in my hands. "I'm sorry," I said through my fingers. "I didn't mean to say that. It came out wrong. What I meant is—"

"Oh, I know what you meant all right," he interrupted. "Loud and clear. You know, I never thought I'd hear it from you."

"Don't get all—"

Again, he didn't let me finish. "I don't need this," he said as he stood up and walked away.

"Dumb me!" I swore.

I tried to speak to Jonathan a few times during afternoon classes, but he ignored me. In science, I tried to stare at him the whole period, waiting for him to glance in my direction. He didn't. He treated me like I was completely invisible.

At three o'clock I waited by his locker, determined to speak to him.

"Why are you standing there, Stormy?" Loreeta wanted to know. "Are you waiting for Jonathan?"

I nodded. "I need to talk to him. I said something I shouldn't have at lunchtime."

"You'll have a long wait," she told me. "He's already left. He seemed to be in a hurry."

44

"In a hurry not to talk to me." I sighed. "Guess I'll try him at home later."

"Don't forget our date," Loreeta said sweetly.

"Date?"

"To work on the science project," she reminded me. "My place after supper." She slipped a piece of paper into my hand. "I drew a map."

"Right." I was upset about Jonathan, but I still managed a decent smile.

I was so preoccupied with how I was going to get Jonathan to accept my apology that I didn't notice the crowd of people around the gym bulletin board as I walked down the hall. I only became aware of the crush when an arm pulled me into the middle of the mob.

"The schedule's up, Stormy. Isn't this exciting? Our team is on the board. *My* team is on the board. The Dregs are official." Joey didn't pause between the sentences.

I studied the game sheet. There were sixteen teams entered in the Mallory Trophy tournament. The schedule was straight elimination. If you lost a game, you were out. Simple enough. Our first game was against a team called the Screaming Eagles. Someone pointed to the member list for that team. "They've won it," a voice said. "Nobody is going to beat them."

I read the names on the list: Dabny Paulty, Adon and Pierce Kobel, Tulip Nixon, Orchid Lang. I had to agree with the voice's opinion.

"Look at the guys on the Dregs," another voice said. "That's got to be a joke. Those guys would never form a team."

One of the kids in my homeroom said, "You're putting us on, Stormy."

I just smiled at him before turning to Joey. "I have to get to the Dungeon."

"I'll walk with you," Joey said.

We squeezed through the crowd, took a quick drink from the water fountain, and headed for the DT Dungeon.

"At least we get to play one game," I noted.

"What do you mean?"

"There's no way we can beat the Screaming Eagles."

"Don't say that," Joey scolded. "You *think* you're going to lose and you do lose. Think positive. We're the Dregs. We're number one."

"I'm still not sure about the name of our team," I told him. "And I *am* being positive. But I'm being realistic too. We're not going to beat the Screaming Eagles."

"What's so good about them?" Joey argued. "Dabny Paulty isn't that good. He may be big, but he's super slow."

I chuckled. "Big counts for a lot. That's why we're happy we have Melvin."

"Dabny won't score any goals," Joey affirmed.

"He won't have to. The Kobel twins will score all they need."

"They're just so-so athletes," Joey said.

"So-so? What planet have you been on for the past few months? Adon was backup quarterback of the junior high football team. Pierce was a running back. That's a major accomplishment for seventh graders. They're the best, Joey."

"It's just that they brag so much, we've started to

believe what they say," Joey said. "I take gym with them. They're not all that hot."

"I take gym with them too. They're the best. So are the Flower Power."

"The Flower Power?" Joey snorted. "They're the weak link on the team."

I just shook my head at that comment. Tulip Nixon and Orchid Lang were the female equivalent of the Kobels. I'd watched them play basketball for the Taft team. They got their nickname, the Flower Power, because of their first names and the way they played guard together.

When we reached the door of the Dungeon, Joey punched my arm. "We can do it, Stormy. I know we're up for this. We just have to . . . what the heck?"

The outside door flew open. I recognized Jonathan silhouetted by the sunlight. What was he doing coming back into the school? And why was he holding his hand over his face? He staggered through the doorway, swayed off balance, and slumped against the wall.

I rushed over to him. "What's wrong?"

He answered with a gurgly moan. Tears streamed from his eyes. Blood flowed through his fingers. "He's not going to get away with this," Jonathan moaned. "I won't let him get away with it."

Mr. Waddell rushed out of the Dungeon and pushed us aside. He ordered me into the room, Joey out of the school, and took an unsteady Jonathan down to the office. I watched them until they disappeared, then stepped into the Dungeon.

Dimps broke into her mess of dimples when she saw me. "Hi, Storkee."

47

"Hey, Dimps. How's it going?"

"I fine. Why yu mad?"

"I'm not mad," I answered. "Something happened to Jonathan. I'm worried about Jonathan."

"Kevin happened to Jonathan," Amber said as she entered the Dungeon. She didn't bother to sit down.

"What do you mean?" I asked.

"I mean Kevin Paulty smashed Jonathan in the face," Amber explained. "He waited for Jonathan outside and just pounded him. There was no reason for it, Stormy."

"The reason was he didn't pay for protection," I said. "The Terminators make us pay a quarter a day for . . ." I stopped when I noticed mascara-black tears sliding down Amber's cheeks. "Amber? What's wrong? Are you hurt or something?"

She looked up and wiped the tears into a smudge of blackness. "Why do people do that to each other? Why does somebody want to hurt somebody else?"

"I don't know," I said. "If I could figure that out, I'd be able to help a lot of people, wouldn't I?"

A smile flickered at the corner of her lips. "You know, Stormy, you're a nice person."

"I am?"

She nodded. "Both you and Jonathan are. Look, I just came to tell Waddell, I can't stay today. I have to get home. Will you tell him?"

"Sure."

The flicker became a real smile. "Thanks, Stormy. Sorry about the waterworks."

"Hey," I said, "no problem."

She walked out of the room.

"Why Amker cry?" Dimps wanted to know.

"I don't know," I answered. "I don't know."

* * *

I called at Jonathan's house after my DT. There was nobody home. That worried me. I wondered if his father had taken him to the hospital. There *was* an awful lot of blood. I wouldn't be surprised if his nose was broken.

I picked up Brandon from Mrs. Kellock's. "Would it be possible for you to watch Brandon for a couple of hours after supper?" I asked Mrs. Kellock.

"Why not?" she agreed. "I'm not going anywhere and little Jessica enjoys the company. Do you have to go out?"

"I'm going to Loreeta's house to work on a science project," I told her.

"Loreeta?" Mrs. Kellock winked at me. "Well, since this is in the name of romance, I'd be doubly pleased to baby-sit Brandon."

I felt myself blush. "It isn't like that," I tried to explain. "She's just a friend."

"Whatever you say, Stormy." Mrs. Kellock winked at me again.

I took Brandon home and began cooking chili Hamburger Helper. Brandon sat at the kitchen table drawing pictures of vegetables in his sketchbook.

"Why do you do that?" I asked. "You're the only kid in the whole world who likes to draw pictures of potatoes and bean sprouts."

"So?"

"So draw something normal. Draw aliens. Draw pictures of people being eaten by werewolves. Draw traffic accidents."

"Yuck."

"It doesn't matter if you like drawing that stuff or

49

not. Teachers, parents, and other kids expect it. You'll get labeled as a doze if you continue to sketch vegetables." I pointed at his illustration. "What is that anyway?"

"It's a rutabaga." Brandon beamed proudly.

"A rutabaga? What in heaven's name is a rutabaga?"

"A Swedish turnip," Brandon announced. "Everybody knows that."

"Right," I said. "Everybody."

"Who's this Loreeta girl you were talking to Mrs. Kellock about?"

"Just a girl from my homeroom." I drained the fat out of the pan and added the macaroni, sauce mix, and water.

"She your girlfriend?"

"Just a friend."

"You gonna kiss her and stuff?" he asked.

"No, of course not," I answered.

"Why not?"

I thought about it. I didn't have a good answer. "Because. Don't be a donkey. Let's talk about something else. What did you learn at school today?"

"Nothing," he answered.

"You go to school every day and every day you learn nothing?"

"That's right," he said.

"Supper will be ready in a few minutes." I turned down the heat, stirred the food a few times, and sat at the table opposite Brandon. "So what do you do in school when everybody but you is learning something?"

"I draw vegetables. Can I have a dime?"

"What do you need a dime for?"

"For Darry," Brandon said as he colored the top half of the rutabaga purple.

"Why do you need to give Darry a dime?"

"So he won't beat me up," Brandon said matter-of-factly. "It's worth it. It's just a dime."

"That little gangster. He's doing what his brothers do. Where does he get off?" I was indignant. Nobody had the right to do this to my little brother. "The nerve of the little twerp. I should drop by your school and bomp him one."

"Darry said if I got my older brother after him, he'd get his older brothers after you."

I was so upset the only thing I could do was huff.

"How come you're so mad, Stormy?" Brandon puzzled. "Darry said you pay his brother a quarter a day so you won't get pounded out. A dime is better than a quarter. I think it's best to pay."

A nauseous centipede wriggled around in my stomach.

"What's the matter?" Brandon asked. "You kind of look sick, Stormy."

Oh, no, I thought. Brandon is growing up just like me.

7.

Do You Want to Kiss Me?

I tried phoning Jonathan after supper, but all I got was Mr. Stewart's recorded voice on the machine. I left a message asking Jonathan to call me as soon as he got in. Then I realized I probably wouldn't be around to get it, since I was going to Loreeta's.

I dropped Brandon at Mrs. Kellock's and followed Loreeta's map to a small bungalow near the mall. I stood at the end of her driveway and took a long, deep breath. It wasn't just to ease my nervousness about visiting Loreeta at home.

I was worried about Jonathan. Was he okay? And I was concerned about Amber too. Heck, I was even a little concerned how Joey would act after we lost our first game to the Screaming Eagles. The Dregs were so important to him.

The Dregs. What a terrible name for us. I should never have agreed.

"Oh, well," I said to myself. "Try to forget about things for a while. You're going to spend some quality time with Loreeta Simpson."

I walked up to Loreeta's front door and rang the bell. A little kid, Brandon's age, swung open the door, gave me a quick look-over, then shouted, "He's here!" over his left shoulder.

"Hello," I said. "I'm Stormy. I've come to see Loreeta."

"I know who you are," the little kid smirked. "All I been hearing about is you."

"Really?"

Loreeta appeared behind him and gave him a tender slap on the head. "Invite Stormy in, Brett," she scolded.

"Come in," Brett said.

I did as I was told, slipping off my Reeboks.

"You don't have to take off your shoes," Loreeta said.

"It's a habit."

"He's not so skinny," Brett announced. "You said he was really skinny."

Loreeta blushed a little. "I didn't say *really* skinny," she defended. Then she said to me, "I was trying to describe you to my family."

After Loreeta took my jacket, Brett grabbed the sleeve of my sweatshirt and escorted me into the family room to meet Mrs. Simpson. She shook my hand and welcomed me. Then she made a not-so-secret wink at her daughter, which caused Loreeta to blush again.

"Mr. Simpson works at the plant," she told me. "He's on afternoons this week. Maybe you can meet him next time you visit."

I explained about my parents working the same shift and how I took care of Brandon.

Mrs. Simpson seemed impressed to hear it. "That's very responsible of you."

"Let's go to my room and get started, Stormy," Loreeta suggested. Then she glared at her brother. "You bug us and you're road kill."

"Loreeta," her mom objected, "I hate it when you talk like that. It's disgusting."

I tried not to smile.

"Sorry," Loreeta apologized.

"I'll make sure Brett doesn't bother you," Mrs. Simpson said.

Loreeta tugged on my arm. "This way."

"Nice meeting you," I said to her mom.

She smiled. "You too. I'll bring some milk and brownies in a little while."

Loreeta pointed to a large easy chair in the corner of her room. "You can sit there." She sat at her desk. "Families," she grumbled. "Aren't they embarrassing?"

I nodded, even though my family had never embarrassed me, and checked out her room. There were posters of teenage boys on the walls. I recognized some of them from TV shows, but I didn't know their names. On the other side of the room was a large wooden dresser covered with girl things—brush and mirror, makeup, stuff like that. Her desk was made out of the same color wood. There was an expensive-looking computer on the top, flashing the words *Science Project*. Her bed was covered with a frilly, pink spread, loaded with a dozen different-sized Garfields.

"I like him," Loreeta said when she saw me looking at them.

"He's funny," I agreed.

"I'm sorry about Brett," she said. "I didn't say you were *really* skinny, honest. I was just trying to describe you to my folks."

"That's okay. You have to tell the truth. I got short-changed when they were handing out muscles."

"How would you describe me to your parents?" she wanted to know.

"I'd tell them you had a big mouth," I answered. Stupid thing to say.

"A big mouth?" Loreeta didn't know whether to be hurt or angry.

"No, no, no." I tried to recover. "It's *big*, yes, but not in the sense that it's *huge*. I mean, you don't have a *gigantic* mouth. It's powerful and full of dignity."

"Huh?"

"Jeez, Loreeta, I'm saying dumb stuff because I'm nervous. What I'm trying to say is you have a great smile. When you smile the whole room lights up."

"It does?" She sounded happy.

"I don't lie," I insisted, "about anything."

"Would you like to kiss me?" she asked.

The muscles in my back tightened. "Pardon?"

"Would you like to kiss me?" she repeated.

"Kiss you?" My words drooled out of my mouth, mumbly and wet.

"I figure you wouldn't have come over if you didn't like me," she said. "I like you, Stormy."

"You do?"

"Of course. I don't invite people I dislike into my room. That wouldn't make sense, would it?"

"I guess not." I was still having trouble talking.

"If a boy and a girl like each other, sometimes they kiss, right?"

"I guess."

"Well, rather than waiting until you go home, I thought we should get it out of the way now," she reasoned. "That way we'll be able to work on the science project without wondering if we're going to kiss when you go home. Make sense?"

"Yes," I said.

"Then you can kiss me," she announced. She closed her eyes, tilted her head slightly, and puckered her lips.

"You want me to come over there and kiss you?"

She nodded.

I stood up, walked slowly toward the desk, bent over, and gave Loreeta a quick peck on the lips. Her eyes opened quickly. "That's not a kiss. That's what you do to your little brother when you say good night. Kiss me again and this time hold it for a while."

"Okay, but I have a confession first," I admitted. "I've never, ever done this before."

She looked more than surprised, bordering on shocked. "Really?"

"I told you I don't lie."

She nodded. "I thought you'd had lots and lots of girlfriends. Pierce told me you had the reputation of being a cool dude with girls."

"Pierce Kobel?"

She nodded again.

"He's lying. I guess he thought it was a funny joke to have you think I was a big-time mover. He and Adon probably got a chuckle out of it."

"Why would he do that?" she wondered.

"He gives me a hard time."

She stared up at me, studying my face. I wondered if she'd suddenly understood what a clown I was. "I didn't have any reason not to believe him. You're good-looking and you're really funny."

I stared down at her with no idea what I should do next.

"To tell you the truth," she said, "I'm really nervous too. I've never kissed a boy before."

It was my turn to be confused. "But you act like you know what you're doing."

"It's just that—an act. I didn't want you to think I . . . you know, hadn't kissed someone before."

Holy, I thought. This romance stuff sure is complicated.

"You still want to try it?" Loreeta asked.

"A kiss? Yeah, I'd like that a lot."

She closed her eyes and puckered again. I bent over, pressed my lips against hers, and closed my eyes too. It felt neat, warm and soft. Her bottom lip was twitching ever so slightly, like she was nervous. Then I realized it was my lip that was twitching. I didn't know how long I should hold it, so I counted to ten in my head, then pulled away.

When I opened my eyes, she was smiling at me. "Do it again," she said.

So I did. Three more times.

"I guess we should work on science," she said finally. "My mom will be bringing us a snack soon. I don't know how she'd react if she found us kissing instead of working."

I hadn't thought of that. I quickly returned to the easy chair and rubbed my cheeks to wipe off any guilty look. I had an image of Mrs. Simpson catching us and screaming, *"Aaargh!* Bring me a rope. We're going to string this varmint up from the street lamp. He kissed my precious little Loreeta."

I shook the thought away as Loreeta turned her chair to face her computer. She continued to look at me. "Before we start, tell me one thing you like about me." A pause. "Other than my big mouth, that is."

"Your hair," I told her. "I like the way it changes color. It's a different shade of purple every day of the week."

"It's a rinse. It washes out after a couple of days. My mom doesn't like it at all. She says I look too weird. But I thought it would be fun to start Taft School with a different image. Sort of cyberpunk."

"It suits you," I complimented. "What was your image in Canada?"

"I was a jock."

"No?" I doubted. "No way."

"Way." She started counting on her fingers. "I was on the girls' basketball team, volleyball team, floor hockey team, track team, swim team, and gymnastics team."

"You should tell people. You'd be an instant hit with the Flower Power."

"That's why I'm trying an alternate look. I knew all kinds of kids like Tulip and Orchid at my other school. I wanted to meet other kinds of people. And I have. I've met you. And that makes me happy."

"Maybe you should listen to your mom," I said. "If people think you're weird, you get picked on."

"Then they're morons," she asserted. "That's what I like about you, Stormy. You're so different."

"You like that?"

"I knew I was going to like you the day I saw you painting your fingernails with Liquid Paper in math. It was such a quirky thing to do. It was so neat."

"I wanted to see what it looked like," I explained.

"I knew I had to talk to you the day you sewed

your finger to the pillow case you were making in home ec.," she went on.

"That was an accident. It really hurt. I felt like a total fool."

She laughed. "You should have seen your face when you called to Mrs. Rozelle, 'Excuse me, ma'am. I think I've done something wrong.' What a hoot."

"You thought that was funny?"

"And cute too."

"Yeah?"

"But I knew I wanted you as my boyfriend when you and Jonathan got the rubber cement in art and spread it on the table."

I felt suddenly embarrassed.

"Remember that? You let it dry, then you started rolling it into little balls." She began laughing again. "And you and Jonathan pretended they were boogers and started flicking them at each other. That was hysterical. I haven't done that since third grade."

"We got a free visit to the Dungeon for it. Mrs. Ford told us it was gross. She called us childish and immature." I recited the assistant principal's lecture.

"Mrs. Ford has no sense of humor," she declared.

I thought about Jonathan pulling fake boogers out of his nose, and soon Loreeta wasn't the only one laughing. I chuckled up a storm too. It was funny, in a gross, childish-type way, but it was still funny.

"This is really strange," I said. "I was scared you wouldn't like me because I was so unusual. I say and do stupid things at the wrong times. I never, ever imagined someone would like me because of it. I never imagined someone would think they were funny."

59

"It's everybody else's problem if they don't know how to laugh," Loreeta concluded. "Let's get to work or we won't even decide on a topic before you have to leave. What do you think we should do our project on?"

I hesitated, reluctant to ask the next question, in case I didn't like the answer. "A few moments ago, you said you wanted me as your boyfriend. Do you still mean that?"

"Of course," she said. "You're here, aren't you? And we did kiss five times. That officially makes you my boyfriend."

Fate was sure roaring down my life's highway in overdrive.

8.

Strange Phone Calls

I kissed Loreeta for a sixth time when we said good night. We must have held our mouths together for nearly thirty seconds. This time my bottom lip didn't shake.

Despite the fact we talked about our families, our old elementary schools, how Burlington, Canada, and Burlington, Vermont, were a little different and a lot the same, and lots of other personal stuff, we got a fair amount of work done on the science project. We chose *Fossil Plants* as our topic. With the help of the Simpson's encyclopedia and what we already knew from the books we'd read, we zipped along. Loreeta's computer has an awesome graphics program and she designed a couple of terrific diagrams. I was positive we'd get a good mark.

I picked up Brandon, made him take a bath, and tucked him in. "So you don't think I should pay Darry a dime?" he asked before I switched off the light.

"No way," I affirmed. "That's the last thing you do. You do that and Darry thinks of you as a loser for the next five years. You'll hit junior high and still be paying the little creep."

"What should I do then?"

"Let me sleep on it," I answered. "I'll give you an answer in the morning."

"Okay, Stormy. Good night."

I flicked the light, headed for the phone, and tried Jonathan. He answered, sounding stuffy and tired.

"Jonathan," I said. "It's me, Stormy."

"I got your message," he said in a monotone. "I called about an hour ago and nobody was home. What do you want?"

"Don't hang up, okay? I'm really, really sorry about what I said at lunch. All I was trying to say is that you're a lot like me. I didn't mean it to come out that way. Honest. You know how I say stupid things. I don't think that way. You have to believe me."

There was silence on the other end of the phone. For a moment, I thought he might have hung up, but I heard him breathing.

"I've learned a lot in the last few hours, Jonathan," I continued. "What Kevin did to you has taught me something. Brandon has taught me something. And Loreeta taught me something too."

"Loreeta?"

I smiled. He couldn't hide the surprise and curiosity in his voice.

"I kissed her," I bragged. "More than once."

"You kissed Loreeta Simpson? When? How?"

"Before I tell you, I want to hear you say you accept my apology. I want to know we're still best friends."

"I suppose so." He sounded less than enthusiastic.

"Is that a *yes?*"

"Yes. Tell me about Loreeta."

So I did. When I was finished, his comment was,

"It's hard to believe you're not making it up, Stormy."

"My luck has changed," I said. "But Loreeta and I aren't what's important. Tell me about you. How's your nose?"

"Sore," he said. "But it's not broken. Did you hear what happened?"

"Kevin the Barbarian was waiting for you outside the school."

"That's right. . . ." Jonathan went on to tell me how Kevin and a group of Terminators walked up to him on the sidewalk in front of Taft. Kevin demanded his protection money; Jonathan refused. So Kevin started pushing him around. Finally, he planted a right hook directly into the center of Jonathan's face.

"Ouch," I said.

"We reported him to the police," Jonathan said. "That's assault. He's not allowed to touch me. My dad said it was the right thing to do."

"The police? The police are going to get involved in what junior high kids do? You really meant it when you said he wasn't going to get away with it."

"But he is," Jonathan said. "The police can't do anything. It's my word against Kevin's. He says he didn't do it. And he's got a couple of witnesses who told the police he was already at the arcade the same time he was supposed to be attacking me."

"So what are you going to do?" I asked. "You going to pay him the money you owe?"

"I don't *owe* him anything." Jonathan's voice got shaky, but it wasn't because he was scared. He was angry. "Of course, I'm not going to pay! He can beat on me every day. I won't pay anymore."

I didn't know what to say. I wanted to help Jonathan, but what he was doing was almost like a form of I-want-to-get-beat-up-suicide. Common sense says there has to come a point when you stop being brave and dopey and become wimpy and smart.

No, that wasn't right. Everything Jonathan had said, *was saying*, was true. He shouldn't have to pay. It was wrong. I thought about Brandon. It was wrong for my brother too.

So why was it right for me?

It was time for me to stand up for myself.

"I'm with you all the way, Jonathan," I announced, more bravely than I felt. "Kevin will have to beat both of us up because I've just handed over my last silver George Washington."

Again there was silence on the other end of the phone.

"Jonathan? You still there?"

"You mean it?"

"I think so."

"You think?"

"I mean it," I said. I added *I think* in my head.

"Thanks, Stormy. I'm sorry I got mad at you this afternoon. You're a good friend. You and me together, huh?"

Even if we face the same firing squad, I thought.

I was brushing my teeth, getting ready for bed when the phone rang. I did a fast spit, ran into the kitchen, and picked it up. "Hello."

"Hi, Stormy. It's Joey."

"What's up?"

"I've been calling you all evening," he told me.

"I was out."

"Listen, I just wanted to tell you Mr. Woloski phoned me to ask if we'd like some practice time tomorrow. I said, 'You bet.' We have to work on our team chemistry. We have to mesh as a well-oiled unit. We have to develop a potent offense. We have to solidify into an impenetrable defense. We have to—"

"What time is practice?"

"Tomorrow morning at eight-thirty in the small gym. We have it for the whole half hour before first bell."

"Okay, I'll be there."

"Super. That means everybody will make it. Except Melvin. He's got something else to do. And I don't think Amber wants to get up that early. But Dimps will be there. Maybe. She had a hard time understanding what I was saying. But you and me for sure. We'll be able to work on our passing."

"See you tomorrow, Joey."

"Right. Hey, Stormy?"

"What?"

"Go to bed. You shouldn't be up so late. You need all the sleep you can get so you have enough energy for the game on Friday. You don't want to bag out halfway through, do you?"

"Stop talking to me then."

"Oh."

"Good night, Joey."

I'd just hung up the phone when it rang again. "What did you forget, Joey?"

"Huh? I want to speak to Stormy."

I recognized Dabny Paulty's voice. What was he doing calling me?

"It's me," I answered.

"Good," Dabny said. "I got you at last. Listen, I got two things. First, you have got to talk to your idiot friend or else he's going to be neck deep in you know what. Tell Jonathan to smarten up."

I didn't respond.

"My brother is losing his patience."

"What's the other thing?" I asked.

"The other thing is I notice we play your team, the Dregs, in the first game of the Mallory Trophy tournament on Friday. What's the Dregs anyway? That some kind of joke?"

"We like it," I lied.

"I don't think you got any chance to beat us," Dabny went on. "But you got Melvin. And Joey is kind of fast, and, well, maybe there could be a couple of fluke goals or something. I want you to understand I'm not going to be too happy if we lose. You know what I'm saying?"

I translated. "You want me to play lousy so you guys are sure to win."

"Exactly. You're pretty intelligent, Stormy."

"You know something, Dabny?" I said, again more brave than I felt. "You sound incredibly simple-minded."

"What?"

This is for you, Jonathan, I thought as I pictured Dabny Paulty sitting in his home in a muscle shirt, flexing his biceps, and getting ready to eat something raw.

"You sound like a gangster from an old black-and-white movie," I went on. "Completely dim-witted."

"You're cruising for a bruising, Stormy," he threatened.

And this is for you, Brandon.

I laughed louder. *"You're cruising for a bruising,"* I mocked. "Don't you realize how much of a bozo you sound? Get a life, Paulty."

"You and me are going to have a little private meeting at school tomorrow," he snarled.

I was aware of my heart pounding like a canary in a microwave. My grip on the receiver was slipping because of my sweating palms. *Do you really know what you're doing here?* the little voice in my head said.

"I don't want to talk to you anytime, anywhere," I shot back. "Don't come around asking me for any more quarters because from now on I'm like my best friend, Jonathan. I'm not going to pay you either. You got that?" Then after a moment, I added, "Fathead."

"Tomorrow." Dabny said the word as if it had eight syllables instead of three—dragged-out, sort of like a long growl.

I took a shower, squeezed a little pimple on my chin, and studied the hair on my upper lip in the bathroom mirror. It was definitely getting darker. If I squinted and used a little imagination, I could almost see a mustache. Then for a few horrible seconds I imagined my features after Dabny and the Terminators got ahold of me. I'd better think of a plan for me and Brandon.

The phone rang for the third time. As I picked up the receiver, I checked the stove clock. It was late. My parents would be home in a half hour. I was supposed to be in bed.

"Stormy?" It was a girl's voice. For a moment, I thought it was Loreeta. "Is that you, Stormy?"

"Amber?"

"Hi. Yes, it's me."

Amber Littlewood calling me? Talk about strange phone calls.

"Can I talk to you, Stormy?" Amber asked.

"I guess. It's kind of late though."

"Oh, I don't want to talk now. Tomorrow at school?"

"Why do you want to talk to me?"

"I'll tell you tomorrow. When's a good time?"

"How about before our floor hockey practice at eight-thirty?" I suggested.

"I can't. That's too early."

"You like to sleep in?"

"No. I've got to get my brothers off to school. How about lunchtime?"

"Okay."

"Sit at the table where you usually sit," she instructed. "And make sure Jonathan is there too. Thanks, Stormy, it's important."

For the second night in a row, I had a hard time falling asleep. What a day. I'd insulted my best friend. Made up with him. Stood up for him. Kissed a girl for the first time. Kissed Loreeta Simpson's wonderful lips. Insulted the seventh grade tough guy. Probably got the whole school gang looking for me. Who could sleep after all that?

And don't forget Amber. That was a mystery. What did she want to talk about?

9.

Melvin and Dimps

I woke up to the first heavy snowfall of winter. It was thick and wet, a usual early December dump. It fell in lazy flakes, the size of postage stamps, making it hard to see across the street.

Before leaving, I told Brandon, "Look, I thought about your problem with Darry and my problem with his older brothers. Here's what you have to do. . . ."

"What a great plan," Brandon said when I was finished. "I hope I can remember everything you told me."

I handed him three dimes. "Write it down if you have to. Just remember your crazy relatives and let your imagination go."

Brandon nodded. "It's perfect. Thanks, Stormy. You going to do the same thing to his brothers?"

"Dabny is going to be in for a surprise," I answered.

I tromped to school, wishing I'd searched for my winter boots when my sneakers got soaked. Every so often I twirled around, checking up and down the street to make sure I wasn't about to run into Dabny or any of the other Terminators. I didn't really expect to meet anybody, since it was so early. So it was a surprise when I saw the snowy form of Melvin Hardtack walking the other way, carrying his gym bag. He appeared to be heading for the local strip mall.

"Hey, Melvin," I shouted. "You're going the wrong way. School's this way. You lost in the blizzard?"

As I got closer, I could tell he wasn't happy to see me. "Hello, Sprague," he grunted.

"Stormy," I told him. "My name's Stormy. Or you can call me Stormalong. I don't care which." I tapped his gym bag. "You've decided to practice floor hockey after all?"

"I'm not going to school. I'm going someplace else."

"With a gym bag?"

"Yeah, with a gym bag," he grunted. "You got a problem with that, Sprague?"

"Stormy," I reminded him as I glanced over his shoulder. *Where's Melvin going?* I thought. I peered at the snow-fuzzed signs in the strip mall.

The 7-Eleven? No, he wouldn't need a gym bag in there. Unless he was going to rob the place. Could he . . . *naw.*

The beauty salon?

"What are you laughing at, Sprague?" Melvin demanded. "You laughing at me?"

"It's Stormy. And, of course, I wasn't laughing at you," I fibbed. "I was just thinking of a joke."

Tae Kwon Do Academy? That fit.

"You going to the karate place?" I asked.

"I . . . I . . . no, and it's not karate. It's different."

"How would you know it's different unless you've been there? You take kung fu, don't you?"

He chewed on his bottom lip for a few moments.

"Yeah, I take Tae Kwon Do lessons. Don't tell anybody though. You tell anyone and I'll get mad."

"Why?"

"Just 'cause."

"Oh, I get it. You want it to be a secret so the next time you get in a fight, you can completely change somebody's face into chow mein."

"You think that?" Melvin asked.

"What other reason can there be?"

"Then you're crazy!" he snapped. He reached over, grabbed the collar of my jacket, and twisted it, pulling me up so I had to balance on my toes. "You got to promise you won't tell nobody. I take class every morning with the adults so nobody at school knows, and I want to keep it that way."

"Okay," I croaked. "You're strangling me."

He looked at his hand as if he didn't know he was crushing my windpipe and let go. "Sorry, Sprague."

"Ow!" I rubbed my neck. "Ow, ow, ow! Is that any way to treat your floor hockey teammate who's name is Stormy?"

"I said I was sorry."

"So what's up, Melvin?" I wanted to know. "Why is it a big secret? Why else would you take karate if you weren't planning to annihilate an army?"

"It's not karate. It's Tae Kwon Do. It's different. They're teaching me discipline and how to meditate."

"Meditate? You mean, where you cross your legs, close your eyes, and think of flowers and birds and junk?"

"Not quite," he said. "But kind of. I'm cold. I'm going inside. Remember, don't tell nobody."

I grabbed the sleeve of his jacket to stop him. "Just a sec. Why do you need to meditate?"

He sighed, reluctant to tell me. "I'm cold."

"Me too. But this is fascinating. Come on, Melvin. If you don't explain, I'll die of terminal curiosity."

"It's to help my temper," he said. "Once upon a time I used to be a real bully."

"Tell me about it," I said. "I remember in fifth grade you bopped me in the nose. It bled on and off for a whole week. There isn't a guy I know who hasn't been dumped on by you."

The little voice was asking, *Should you really be saying this to the meanest, baddest dude in seventh grade?*

"You're the meanest, baddest dude in seventh grade," I declared.

"That's why I'm taking Tae Kwon Do," he said.

"So you can be meaner and badder?"

"I'm taking it . . ." He sighed. "I'm taking it so people will like me. There. Satisfied?"

I was confused. "Like you? You learn how to kick someone in the head and they like you?"

"I got to go."

I followed him across the parking lot. "Explain it to me, Melvin."

"Why?"

" 'Cause I'm not all that bright and I want to know."

He stopped. "Sure they teach you how to kick someone in the head. But they also teach you discipline. When you meditate, you learn how to control your feelings. Have you noticed I don't pick on people anymore?"

"That's right," I said. "I haven't seen you lose your temper in months."

"Tae Kwon Do helps me stay cool," he went on. "I

knew hitting people wasn't making me popular, but I couldn't stop it. And I'd get mad at myself because I couldn't stop. Understand?"

"I think so. That's what you were doing in the Dungeon the other day. When you got angry at what I said, you had your eyes closed and you were breathing slow. You were meditating."

"Right. I got so frustrated with myself that I went to see Mr. Walker, the guidance counselor. He suggested I take some kind of martial art. He said they would teach me how to control my anger. He was right. I'm never going to hurt anybody anymore. It's like I told the Terminators when they asked me to join their gang. I'm never going to pick on anybody for the rest of my life."

"The Terminators wanted you?"

"They pick on people."

"Incredible," I said. "Just when I think I've had the two most interesting days of my life, the next day starts out just the same."

He looked at his watch. "I'm late."

"Why don't you skip it for today?" I suggested. "Come practice floor hockey with us. We play our first game tomorrow."

He thought about it for a moment. "No, I better not. Promise you won't tell anybody?"

"Okay," I answered. "If that's what you want."

"Thanks, Sprague."

"Stormy."

"You know something," he told me. "You got a funny name."

"My mom was looking for something different. She named me after a sea captain in an old poem."

"It's funny, but it's you. You want to be buddies?"

I took a step backward. Melvin Hardtack wanted to be my friend? The day was getting more incredible by the second.

"You know what it's like not to have any friends, Sprague?"

I nodded. "Sure. I don't have any friends."

"You and Jonathan are friends," he pointed out.

"Okay, I've got *one* friend."

"I don't," he said. "I've got nobody. So what do you say? Friends?"

"I'd rather be your friend than your enemy," I answered.

He slapped me on the shoulder.

"Ow! Does this mean you won't steal my lunch anymore?" I asked.

The smile turned into a frown. "I don't steal. I only eat what you don't want. I only take what you're going to throw away."

"Sometimes. But sometimes we just let you have it because we're scared. Nobody is going to refuse you."

"I never thought of that. I was just hungry."

"Well, from one friend to another, I think you should stop it."

He thought for a moment. "Maybe that's a good idea. But I'll sure feel hungry. I guess I'll have to pack a bigger lunch. I'll see you, Sprague."

"Stormy. One last thing, Melvin. The other day in the Dungeon when you agreed to be on Joey's team, it was because of Amber Littlewood, wasn't it? You really like her, don't you?"

He shifted, a little embarrassed. "Amber's okay. But Dimps is a lot cuter. I really like Dimps."

"Dimps? Incredibler and incredibler!" I gasped.

"Stormy," Joey called when I walked into the small gym. "Glad to see you. I thought you'd forgot. You're five minutes late."

"Believe it or not, I was talking to Melvin," I said. "And I had to change into my shorts. It looks like I didn't miss anything."

Dimps was standing next to Joey, holding an upside-down floor hockey stick. "You're just in time to help me teach Dimps," Joey said. "I don't think she's ever played floor hockey before."

"What was your first clue?" I asked.

Joey twisted the stick in Dimps's hands. "It goes this way," he explained.

Dimps nodded. "Kes."

Joey bobbed his head. "Kes. Kes." He pointed at the stick. "This is a floor hockey stick."

"Dis iz a fur hooky sick," Dimps mimicked.

"Right," Joey said. "See, Stormy, she'll catch on in no time." Joey held up the plastic puck. "This is a floor hockey puck," he told Dimps.

"Diz iz a fur hooky duck."

Joey waved the puck in Dimps's face. "Not the duck. The puck."

Dimps nodded. "Da duck."

"Much better," I noted.

Joey pointed to the far end of the gym. "That's the net, Dimps. The whole idea of the game is to put this puck in the other team's net." He waved the puck again. "While you stop the other team from putting this puck in your net."

"I peg my bardon."

I tried to help out. "We want to score a goal."

Dimps nodded. "We wont to scare a mole."

75

Joey flashed me a frustrated what-am-I-going-to-do look.

"She's got that dictionary," I suggested. "You know the one which translates English into her language." I looked around the gym and saw her books piled on a bench. I noticed the green and blue cover of her phrase book. I jogged over, picked it up, and jogged back.

I spent a minute searching for a phrase which might help.

"Well?" Joey asked impatiently.

"I can't find anything that fits. Most of it is really stupid. Here's a phrase that says, *Please hold my horse while I climb on.* They're all dumb. Here's another, *Are there any boats to take me deep sea fishing?* Listen to this one, *Can I borrow a wet suit?*"

"There's got to be something." Joey was rocking on his toes and heels, getting more hyper by the second.

"Hey, here's the word for *net*," I said. *"Kolvar."*

"Kes." Dimps grinned and pointed at the net. *"Kolvar."*

Joey grinned and pointed at the net too. "Score a goal in the *kolvar.*"

"Scare a mole in da *kolvar?*" Dimps puzzled.

"Here's the phrase for 'drive in,' " I said. *"Unkos int."*

"We don't want her to drive anywhere," Joey complained. "We want her to shoot the puck with her stick."

" 'Drive in' is sort of like 'shoot at,' isn't it?" I said. "Don't basketball players drive in a two pointer? She'll get the meaning."

"Maybe," Joey said. "Give it a try. Right now, she thinks she's scaring moles."

"Okay," I directed Dimps. "Drive in the net. *Unkos int kolvar.*"

She looked at me as if I had grapefruits growing out of my ears. *"Unkos int kolvar?"*

"Yes," I repeated. *"Unkos int kolvar."*

She stared at me, then at Joey. *"Unkos int kolvar?"*

"You." Joey pointed at her. *"Unkos int kolvar."* He indicated the net.

"Okay, Jokee. I wont to play fur hooky. I wont to scare a mole. I wont, er . . . *unkos int kolvar.*" To our amazement, Dimps dropped her stick and charged full out, headfirst at the net. She lowered her head and dove into the mesh. Her momentum popped the crossbar from the posts and Dimps ended in a tangle of arms and legs and string netting.

"What happened?" Joey exclaimed.

Dimps rolled around on the floor like a trapped fish as the destroyed net tightened around her. We ran over and helped her from the mess. Dimps stood up, a hundred dimples decorating her face. "I scare a mole," she beamed proudly. "I play fur hooky."

What had gone wrong? I checked the page in Dimps's phrase book again. And I found my mistake.

"What are you laughing at?" Joey asked. "What's so funny?"

"I got it figured," I said. "I know why she did it. I read it wrong. *Unkos int kolvar* doesn't mean 'drive in the net.' It means *'dive* in the net.' Silly me, huh?"

"Silly me!" Joey yelled. "That's all you can say?!"

"Hey, there's no need to shout. It was a mistake. A

77

funny mistake. There's no harm done. Dimps isn't hurt. It'll be easy to put the net back together."

"Silly me?!" He pushed me in the chest, hard enough that it hurt. "How about *stupid me!*"

"Joey, it's not a big deal."

"First, Melvin decides he has something better to do. Then Amber doesn't show. Then you get Dimps to dive into the net. What do you think Mr. Woloski is going to say when he sees the net? He'll probably kick us out of the tournament."

"We'll have the net back together in five minutes," I said.

"And how much time will we have to practice? We play our first game tomorrow and we haven't worked out a game plan. We haven't decided who's playing what position. We haven't even practiced a single shot."

"It's not that bad," I observed. "Dimps will really throw off the Screaming Eagles goalie when she *unkos int kolvar.*"

A rush of tears flowed from Joey's eyes. Large rivulets streamed down his face and dripped off his chin. "It wasn't supposed to be like this. This is my team. It wasn't supposed to work out this way."

"It's no big deal," I repeated.

"Yes, it is," he cried as he ran across the gym and into the boys' locker room.

Dimps didn't have a clue what was going on. "Jokee no lick me play fur hooky?"

I searched through the phrase book, but all I found were stupid phrases like, *Will it rain all day?* and *Is there a Ping Pong table in this building?* Finally, I said, "He's not mad at you. He's mad at something else."

"So am I!" someone called.

Two red Terminator jackets walked through the gym doors. Inside them were Dabny and Kevin the Barbarian Paulty.

10.

Intimidation

If Dabny Paulty's description is big and scary, then I'd have to describe his older brother as bigger and scarier. He's Dabny with twenty extra pounds of muscle and fifty extra pounds of nastiness. Over the years, Kevin has perfected his intimidation techniques. He saunters like a giant ape when he walks, swaying his massive shoulders and swinging his thick arms. When he stands, he thrusts his face forward like his neck is vomiting his head. His top lip is bent into a permanent snarl.

When Kevin the Barbarian walked across the gym and stood in front of me, I was a half degree away from a total meltdown.

"Don't punch me in the face," I begged. "Hit me someplace that won't leave a scar."

My plea for mercy surprised him. Little wrinkles formed around his lip snarl. "Punch you? I'm not going to punch you." His voice rumbled, thick and full of gravel.

"You're not?"

Kevin shook his head. "Course, I'm not. Dabny is, but I'm not."

I glanced at Dabny. He stood three feet behind his brother, punching his fist into the palm of his other hand.

"Dabny thinks you were rude to him on the phone last night," Kevin went on. "But that comes in a minute. First, you and me have got to talk about our deal."

"Our deal?"

"You know. You pay us a quarter a day and we stay out of your hair. Dabny tells me you didn't pay yesterday and you said something on the phone about never paying again. That was just a mistake, wasn't it?"

"I g-guess." The *g* stuck in my throat and I stammered.

"You guess?" Kevin scratched the razored *T* on his short-haired scalp. "Does that mean yes or no? Are you going to keep paying us or not?"

I wasn't sure how to answer. *Yes*, it wasn't a mistake. *No*, it was a mistake. *Yes*, I'll pay you. *No*, I won't pay you. What should I say?

I had a 50 percent chance of being right. "Yes."

"Good. That makes me happy." His upper lip didn't relax. "The last thing I need is another puke-faced seventh grader giving me a hard time." Kevin stepped aside. "He's all yours, Bro."

Dabny took two steps forward to get within right hook distance. "What was it you said last night, Stormy? You called me a fathead, didn't you?"

"I . . . er . . . I . . ."

"Is there a problem?" someone called.

Melvin Hardtack joined us. His hair was wet, and snow covered the shoulders of his jacket. He marched up so he was a hand's length away from Dabny's face. "Hi, Sprague," he said. "I changed my mind about floor hockey practice. I decided to come after all." Melvin wasn't looking at me. His unblinking eyes were focused on Dabny's face.

"What's up, Melvin?" Dabny didn't sound so tough all of a sudden. There was no doubt about it. He was scared.

"This guy bugging you, Sprague?" Melvin asked, his eyes still riveted on Dabny.

Dabny didn't let me speak. "There's no problem here, Melvin," he said. "I was just leaving."

"There's no problem, Sprague," Melvin said. "We can still practice. These guys are going now."

Dabny danced backwards, seeking safety behind his brother. Kevin's face was painted with an expression of complete disgust. He was obviously less than impressed with his brother's lack of courage. Kevin turned and whispered a few angry words at Dabny. I couldn't hear all of Dabny's reply, but I did catch, ". . . not going to mess with the Hulk."

Kevin unzipped his red jacket and tossed it to his brother. "You may make Dabny turn chicken, Hardtack, but you don't scare me at all. This seems like a good time to find out if your rep is half as good as everyone thinks it is."

"Wat go on?" Dimps asked.

I'd forgotten she was still in the gym. What did she think of all this? She must be wondering what kind of strange customs her new country had. I took her arm and pulled her away from the heavyweights. "Someone is going to get killed," I told her.

That had to be the logical result of this matchup. Melvin Hardtack and Kevin Paulty face-to-face was a ticket to global destruction. I figured one of them wouldn't be walking away.

"We're not going to fight," Melvin said. "I told you, I don't do that anymore."

"Don't pull that paper tiger dip on me, Hardtack," Kevin threatened. "I'm about to take you out. You can go down like a wimp or a hardnose, but either way you're going down." He raised his fist and flew at Melvin.

I wish I had slow-motion vision so I could have seen what exactly happened. Kevin swung a right hook in the direction of Melvin's face. Melvin didn't duck or flinch. Instead, he raised his arms fast, blocking the punch and somehow grabbing Kevin's hand. The next thing I saw, Melvin had a firm grip on Kevin's fingers with one hand and his thumb with the other hand. He was pressing the thumb back toward Kevin's wrist, and the Barbarian was definitely not enjoying the experience.

"Jeez, Melvin" he shouted. "Stop that. You're breaking my thumb. Ow. Come on, man. That hurts. Ow."

"See, we're not going to fight," Melvin said. "Are we, Paulty?"

"No. Ow! Come on!" Kevin was hopping around, trying to pull away from Melvin, trying to find a more comfortable position for his hand. "No, we're not going to fight. Let go. Please. Help me, Dabny."

Dabny stood like a statue, unmoving.

"You guys are just leaving," Melvin affirmed.

"Yeah, Dabny and me are leaving. Ow. Please. Let go. You're wrecking my thumb."

Melvin released Kevin's hand. "Get lost," he ordered.

Kevin began massaging his wounded thumb. He glanced over at me and got suddenly angry. "What are *you* smiling at!?" he shouted. "Nothing has changed between you and me, Stormy. Melvin can't look out for you all the time."

"Get lost!" Melvin raised his voice twenty decibels.

The Paultys stared at Melvin for a moment, then quickly retreated out of the gym.

Melvin turned to me and smiled. "So, let's play floor hockey, Stormy, my friend."

"You just used my first name," I said.

He threw his arm around my shoulder. "Good friends do that, right?"

It turned out we didn't get any time to play. By the time we reassembled the net, searched in vain for Joey, and taught Dimps how to hold a floor hockey stick, the first bell rang.

"We didn't need the practice anyway," I rationalized.

Joey wasn't in homeroom or in our double English period. At morning break, Loreeta told me, "I saw him getting into a taxi about five minutes before the bell. He seemed really upset."

I explained what had happened in the gym. "He's taking the floor hockey team so seriously. It's important, but it's not the end of the world."

"I've noticed Joey's kind of intense," Loreeta said.

"Maybe he's gone home for the day," I noted. "When he used to get superhyper in sixth grade, he used to go home to calm down."

"I like Joey," she said.

"Me too. And I've learned to like him a lot more in the last few days."

"But I don't like him as much as I like you," she concluded.

We grinned at each other like a couple of Cheetahs from an old Tarzan movie.

"You want to eat lunch with me?" Loreeta asked.

"I can't. I have to meet Amber at lunch."

"Pardon?" Loreeta's features sharpened, which made me feel good because I knew she was jealous.

"She wants to talk to me about something."

"What?"

"I don't know, but she wants to speak to Jonathan too. I'll try to catch her by her locker at the start of lunch. Maybe it won't take long. Then you and me can eat lunch together."

Loreeta smiled. "I'd really like that."

At lunchtime, I headed for Amber's locker. She was keying her combination when I arrived. As soon as she opened the door, half the books fell on the floor. She swore.

"Better not let Waddell hear you say that word," I told her. "You'll be in the Dungeon for sure."

She looked at me, then at the mass of books and paper surrounding her ankles. "Why does this always happen to me?"

"Maybe because your locker is a total mess. I know the symptoms. You should see mine."

"I don't know how it gets that way," she complained.

"I'll give you a hand cleaning up," I said. "Maybe you can tell me what you want to talk about. I kind of have a date for lunch."

"With Loreeta?" Amber asked.

"Yeah. How do you know?"

"Us girls know stuff like that," she said. "Stormy, can I ask you something about Jonathan?"

"Huh? Jonathan Stewart?"

She nodded as she kneeled to pick up her books. I squatted beside her.

"The other day Jonathan asked me to go to a movie with him," she said. "I couldn't because I was busy. Do you think he'll ask again?"

I didn't get a chance to answer. "Here's two of them," a girl's voice said. "Here's two of the Drugs." Four legs flanked us like bookends.

I glanced up to see Tulip Nixon glaring down at me. Tulip has a strange, turned-up nose. It wasn't a big thrill to look directly into her nostrils. Tulip's friend Orchid was standing beside her. It struck me that both halves of the Flower Power had similar nostrils. Part of my mind was amazed how much hair there is in a human nose.

"The Dregs," Orchid corrected. "I think the name really suits them."

"They leave the door to your cage open?" I asked.

The Flower Power ignored my insult.

"We feel it's our duty to tell you you're going to lose tomorrow," Tulip said. "We don't want you to be too disappointed."

"Your team doesn't stand a chance," Orchid added.

Amber stood up, clutching a handful of books and her lunch bag, and regarded the Flower Power. I stood up and leaned against the lockers.

"Don't look so upset, Barbie," Orchid mocked. "It's just the truth."

"The name is Amber," Amber spat through her teeth.

"We know," Tulip interjected. "But it's so easy for

us to forget. Everyone thinks you're pretty, but everyone knows you're empty-headed."

"Don't be nasty, Tulip," Orchid teased. "You're supposed to be kind to dumb animals."

Amber's eyes narrowed into skinny slits. "Will you do me a favor?" she asked the Flower Power. She handed a few books to Tulip and another couple to Orchid. "Will you hold these for a minute, please?"

They looked at Amber. Then at her books. Then at each other. Then at Amber's stuff. Then at each other again. They didn't have a clue what was going on.

Neither did I. *What is Amber up to?* I thought.

Amber reached into her lunch bag and pulled out a package of Twinkies. "I want to share something with you," she said as she ripped the plastic wrap. "That's what my teammate Melvin likes to do with our lunches. He likes to share them."

"What are you—" Tulip began.

"I'm not going to hold your—" Orchid started.

They didn't get a chance to finish because Amber shoved the Twinkies into their faces. With her right hand, she ground cake and cream into Tulip's open mouth. Unfortunately, she wasn't as accurate with her left hand. The Twinkie was smeared up Orchid's nose.

"Have a *treat*," Amber snarled.

"That's a good one," I congratulated.

She winked at me. "Thank you."

The Flower Power dropped the books on the floor and frantically wiped at the goop on their faces.

"You dropped my stuff," Amber said in a hurt tone. "That's not nice. Not after I shared my dessert with you."

The Flower Power made a funny noise, halfway

between a howl and a wail. People in the hallway stopped to look at them. A large audience gathered in a few seconds.

The howl-wail cranked an octave as Tulip and Orchid continued to wipe at the white sugary mess on their faces.

Unfortunately, the commotion attracted the special supervisor of Taft Junior High. Mr. Waddell peered over the crowd, trying to see what wounded animal was making such a frightening noise. He cleared a path through our fellow students, sized up the situation in a second, and pointed his index fingers at Amber and me. "Okay, Miss Littlewood and Mr. Sprague. To the office. Right now. Move it."

11.

You've Always Been Nuts

"But I was just standing there, Mrs. Ford," I explained from the other side of the assistant principal's desk. Mrs. Ford had made Amber wait outside and sent the Flower Power to clean up.

"I find it hard to believe you're innocent, Stormy," Mrs. Ford replied. "If you were that close to this incident, you must have had something to do with it."

"Why would you think that?"

She sang my name. "Stooormyyy."

"Okay, so maybe I have a reputation for doing stupid things, but I didn't have anything to do with washing anyone's face with a Twinkie."

"Are you telling me it was all Amber's fault?" Mrs. Ford probed.

"Not at all. It was the Flower Power's fault," I said. "You should have heard the nasty things they said. They—"

She held up a hand to stop me. "Perhaps I should get this information from the girls. Before I do that, though, I want to discover what Stormalong Sprague's role was."

"I told you, ma'am. I didn't do anything. Honest."

Mrs. Ford arranged some papers on her desk, as if she was killing time while she thought about what to do with me. "You have one day in the Dungeon," she said.

"But I'm innocent, ma'am."

She folded her hands on the desk. "Completely? Let me ask you this, Stormy. Did you try to stop Amber from assaulting Tulip and Orchid?"

I hesitated. "Well . . . no."

"And did you think Amber's deed was humorous?" Mrs. Ford pressed.

"I . . . er . . . it is sort of funny to see someone with a Twinkie sticking out of her nose. Even you'd laugh at that one."

"No, I wouldn't," Mrs. Ford said bluntly. "I'd be horrified. If you don't deserve a DT for aiding and abetting this unfortunate occurrence, then you deserve a detention for having a poor sense of humor."

"Aaaw."

"You may go to lunch now, Stormy. Tell Amber to come in as you leave."

"Yes, ma'am."

"And Stormy."

"Yes, ma'am?"

"I want you to know that your floor hockey team, the Dregs, are the talk of the faculty lounge. All the teachers are pleased you and your teammates have formed a team. We're quite eager to see you play tomorrow. In fact, I plan to be there personally to watch your game."

"Really?"

She nodded. "Best of luck in the tournament."

"You're right," Jonathan agreed. "You didn't deserve a trip to the Dungeon this time. But it was worth it. It sure must have been funny to see the look on the Flower Power's faces. A day in DT is a cheap ticket for that."

"You couldn't see them," I told him as I surveyed the cafeteria. "They were hidden under a layer of cake."

Jonathan laughed, spitting tiny missiles of carrot stick onto the table. I watched Dabny making his rounds of the seventh grade tables, picking up his silver George Washingtons. A fair number of kids were handing over money. The Terminators were making a decent living from their insurance business. Well, the days of Stormalong Sprague's contributions were about to end.

I slipped a quarter under my mug of hot chocolate.

Jonathan watched me as he began work on another carrot wedge. "I thought you hated hot chocolate. I remember making some for you at my house and you refused to drink it."

"I loathe the stuff," I said.

"So why did you buy it?"

"Because it's hot."

"Huh?"

"Sssh. Here comes Dabny."

Dabny Paulty strode over to our table. He made a quick check of the nearby tables, no doubt searching for Melvin. "I want you to know that everything between you and me is cool, Stormy. Because I'm a nice guy, I'm going to forget what you said on the phone last night. I know you say stupid things every once in a while, and last night was just one of those times, right?"

"Whatever you say, Dabny."

"And you are paying us a quarter a day to be our friends. So it's all forgotten."

"Gee, thanks a lot," I said sarcastically.

He didn't press it. Having Melvin as my buddy certainly had its good points.

"Anyway," Dabny said, "it's pay-up time. I trust we aren't going to have any problems today."

"I'm not going to pay you," Jonathan asserted.

"That's right," I added quickly. "He's not going to pay you, but I am. From now on, I'll pay for both of us."

"There's no way you'll do that!" Jonathan thumped the table. "Where would you get such a ridiculous idea?"

While Dabny was watching my best friend, I reached under the mug, gingerly grabbed the quarter and tossed it into the air. "Here's the first payment."

Dabny's big hand snared the coin. It only took a second for him to realize that the quarter was as warm as my hot chocolate mug. He tossed it on the table. "What the—" he shouted.

The coin rattled in a circle as it settled. I made a big production of touching it. By now it was cool, but I snapped my hand away and blew on my fingers. "Yeah, that's the one," I said to Jonathan.

"Why's it so hot?" Dabny demanded.

"My Uncle Charlie's sense of humor," I said. "Don't worry about it. It'll only affect you if you keep it in your pocket for a few hours. That's what they think anyway. Course, they may be wrong."

"What are you talking about?" Dabny asked.

"It's radioactive," I told him. "My crazy Uncle Charlie works at the nuclear power station. Making money radioactive is his idea of a joke. Course, he is . . . crazy."

Dabny looked at me, unsure whether to believe me or not.

"If you put things on top of the reactor and leave them there for a while," I described, "they become radioactive too. That's why it's hot."

Don't pick up the coin, I thought.

"Get out of here," Dabny scoffed. "That's just bull."

"You don't have to believe me. Take the quarter. It'll be sort of an experiment. After I pay you with radioactive quarters for a couple of weeks, we'll see how long it takes you to grow another head."

"That's the dumbest story I've ever heard," Dabny said. "There's no such thing as radioactive quarters."

"So take it," I coaxed.

He moved his arm toward it and stopped. "Give me another quarter," he ordered.

"Okay." I rooted around in my lunch bag and pulled out a pill vial from an old prescription. I'd peeled off the label and inserted one quarter. Then I'd enclosed it in a plastic sandwich bag. I reached across the table and handed the bag to Dabny. He stared at the pill bottle with an expression of complete bewilderment.

"What's this all about?"

"My Aunt Clara's sense of humor," I said. "She works for the Centers for Disease Control in Atlanta. You ever hear of them?"

Dabny nodded. "Yeah."

"She works in the contagious disease section. She smeared that quarter with some strange and exotic virus. Not a fatal one. She won't give you anything that'll kill you, just something that turns you into the Elephant Man."

Dabny scoffed again. "Get off the pot." He began to open the sandwich bag and I stood up with a snap, pushing my chair back.

I grabbed Jonathan's shirt and yanked him to his feet. "We have to be at least five feet away. Aunt Clara said the virus can't travel that far. It'll only infect people standing closer. Like Dabny."

"Get real," Dabny snapped. He may not have believed me, but he stopped opening the bag. "This is a stupid joke. You don't have an uncle who works at the power station or an aunt who messes around with diseases."

"Maybe I don't," I said. "Then again, maybe I do. What are you going to believe?"

Dabny began tapping his forehead. "I'm going to believe you're crazy. You've always been nuts."

I made my best demonic smile, trying to imitate Jack Nicholson in the Stephen King movie, *The Shining*. "That's exactly right, Dabny. I'm crazy. I'm nuts. You know it. Everybody else knows it."

"So give me the money you owe," he demanded.

I reached into my jean's pocket and pulled out a third quarter. I held it by its edge, between the fingernails of my thumb and forefinger. "I'll give it to you. Hold out your hand."

He waffled, extending his hand, then pulling it back. "Why are you holding it that way?"

"No reason," I said. "Then again maybe I painted it with prusaic acid. Who knows?"

"Prusaic acid? What's that?" Dabny asked.

"You don't know?" Jonathan interjected. He'd obviously picked up on my plan and was anxious to play along. "It's a contact poison."

Dabny squinted.

"It seeps through your skin on contact," Jonathan went on. "It gets into your bloodstream and, like they say, the rest is history. You do know what happens to someone with prusaic acid poisoning, Dabny?"

"I'm not going to swallow this BS," he answered.

"Your eyes swell up," Jonathan continued. "They get so big they burst out of their sockets and roll across your face. And you start to throw up. First the food you ate. But that doesn't stop it. You keep puking. People who have touched prusaic acid have thrown up their gallbladders, their spleens, their pancreases, and their livers. Can you imagine how horrible it would be to hork your liver into the toilet, Dabny?"

Gross me out, I thought. "So maybe all this is BS," I said. "But then again, I'm just crazy enough that some, or all, of it is true. I'm so nuts that I can't be trusted, Dabny."

"You don't scare me, jerkface," he gnarled.

"Then take the money," I insisted. "But keep in mind that I might be insane enough to do something totally unpredictable at any time. Is it worth getting Elephant Man's face for a crummy quarter?"

"Or hurling your appendix into the sink?" Jonathan stated.

Dabny spent a few moments looking at us and the quarter in the pill vial. Then he tossed it on the table next to the "radioactive" one. "I don't need this. I've got better things to do than spend time with looney-tunes."

He stomped off, looking for more normal prey.

Jonathan and I shook each other's hands, then high-fived. "What a great idea, Stormy," Jonathan said.

"I thought you were going to blow it," I admitted. "Puking your liver? I figured Dabny would never believe that."

"Why not? He was gullible enough to think the stories about Uncle Charlie and Aunt Clara were true. Radioactive money? Give me a break."

I tried to look as deadly serious as possible. "You thought I was kidding? All the stuff I said about my relatives was true."

"Yeah, and I'm the emperor of China."

"Pleased to meet you, Your Highness."

Jonathan squinted the same way Dabny had. "You can't possibly be telling the truth." Then, after a long pause. "Can you?"

I exploded into laughter. A second later, Jonathan did the same.

12.

Disaster

"So tomorrow's the big day, Mr. Sprague," Mr. Waddell said as I walked into my favorite Dungeon after school. "The Dregs will take to the field of competition and show us the famous Taft determination."

"I don't mean to be rude, sir," I said, "but there's no need for that."

He puffed up for a moment, then relaxed. "I should give you another day for your outburst. But I'm in a good mood today, Mr. Sprague. Just the image of the infamous Dregs of the DT Dungeon attempting to act like a team is making me feel wonderful."

I passed my usual seat and sat next to Amber. She was busy chewing on her pencil and glaring at the special supervisor. I was anxious to speak to her. Mrs. Ford had kept her late at lunchtime, so we hadn't had a chance to talk. I was curious to know why she'd phoned me last night.

"You can stop looking that way immediately, Miss Littlewood," Mr. Waddell ordered.

Amber's expression softened only a little.

"That's better. So how is the team's goalie?" Mr. Waddell asked. "Are your reflexes finely tuned to catch those flying pucks?"

She chewed wood and paint and graphite, trying to keep her temper.

"Enough good-natured bantering," Mr. Waddell decreed. "Let's look busy, people."

Ten minutes later: "I'm going to be busy for a few minutes. I don't want any talking in here while I'm out of the room."

As soon as Mr. Waddell left, Amber closed her science book with a slam. "I wonder what he was like when he was our age. I bet he was a complete jackass."

"He still is," I pointed out. "What did Mrs. Ford give you? How many extra days do you have to spend with Waddell?"

"Mrs. Ford isn't in the same league as Mr. Waddell. She's almost decent," Amber observed. "She only tacked on two DTs, after I catch up on my science, that is. That's not bad considering what I did to the Flower Power."

We surprised the other people in the Dungeon by having a loud, long laugh.

"How come you're so far behind in science?" I wondered. "Your great social life cut into your study time?"

I could tell my comment had upset her. "What? What did I say wrong, Amber? I can tell I said something stupid, but I don't know what."

She sighed. "It's not your fault, Stormy. It's what everybody thinks."

"What does everybody think?"

"That I have some kind of great social life. A couple of girls asked me the other day if I was dating some guy in college. Do you believe that?"

"Are you?"

"Stormy, I'm twelve years old. How do rumors like that start?"

"Maybe because you look eighteen?" I guessed.

"I wish I didn't," she told me. "I wish I was homely or flat chested or something other than me."

I shifted in my seat. Amber talking like that was kind of embarrassing.

"So you think I have a social life?" she went on. "My social life consists of taking care of my little brothers. Do you know what my mom does for a living?"

"No."

"She's a bartender. She works at the Northern Lights on Lincoln Avenue. She starts work at six o'clock in the evening and comes home at three-thirty in the morning. Guess who baby-sits my brothers in the evening and guess who gets them ready for school in the morning?"

"You?"

"Right. My mom is trying to get a job at the plant so she can be home more, but you know how tough it is. Until she does, I'm stuck as full-time baby-sitter. The pits, huh?"

"I had no idea, Amber. I always thought you . . . you know, like the other day when you had the lunch date with Kevin Paulty. I thought that's what your life was like all the time."

"It wasn't a date," she snarled. "I just went for a burger. I'm not even sure why I went. Maybe because he's the first boy at Taft who ever asked me to do anything."

"Wow," I said. "The stuff I'm learning."

"Anyway, Kevin is the reason I wanted to talk to

you and Jonathan at lunchtime. I know what Kevin did to Jonathan yesterday. Jonathan doesn't have to take any guff from Kevin. I know he can't fight back, so I want to help him."

"I don't know what you can do, Amber. The police can't even do anything. They say Kevin can prove he was somewhere else when he was hitting Jonathan."

"Well, I can tell them different," she said firmly. "Remember what I told you yesterday? I saw the whole thing. If Jonathan wants to go to the police or Mrs. Ford or whoever, then I'll be glad to back up his story."

"I'll tell him," I said.

"And while we're at it, why don't we make an appointment to see Mrs. Ford. Let's go tell her how Mr. Waddell behaves in the Dungeon. He shouldn't say the stuff he does."

"Okay," I agreed, feeling suddenly confident. "No more craparoni from anybody."

Disaster struck as we were leaving the Dungeon.

At three-thirty, Mr. Waddell dismissed the DT kids. Amber and I gathered our books and followed the other kids to the door. "I'm looking forward to tomorrow," Mr. Waddell called.

Amber stopped, turned to him, and said, "Me too." Then she said to me, "Do you know if Jonathan is going to dance anywhere in town in the next little while?"

"He dances someplace every weekend," I said. "Why?"

"Because I'd like to watch him."

"This may sound like a stupid question, Amber. But do you like Jonathan?"

"Course, I do," she answered. "This is the second time I've dropped a hint. Tell him, okay? Tell him to phone me again. Tell him I'd love to see a movie with him. But it'll have to be a matinee."

"I'll do that right away," I said.

Amber smiled and walked out the Dungeon door. And collided with a charging Joey Floozeman.

It was the mother of all collisions. Joey bowled into Amber with the force of a herd of runaway musk ox. There was a queer mix of sounds, a *thadump* and a *crack,* followed by a groan and moan. They bounced off each other like opposite magnetic poles and crashed to the floor with a sickening thud. Joey thrashed about on the tiles, a siren sound gurgling from his lungs. Amber lay in a heap, unmoving.

Joey's arm got scrunched under his body when he fell. I tried to comfort him as he complained about how much his wrist hurt. It didn't seem to be sticking at a weird angle, so I figured it probably wasn't broken. While I was telling Joey he was going to be all right, Mr. Waddell tried to revive Amber. She'd been knocked out cold. It took thirty seconds before she regained a groggy form of consciousness. Five minutes later she still didn't seem all that sure where she was.

"Call me and let me know how you are," I told Joey as Mr. Waddell and a few other teachers helped him and Amber into a car and to the hospital.

"So that's it for the Dregs," Joey told me on the phone after supper. "My wrist is too badly sprained. There's no way I can play. I shouldn't have been running in the school. I just wanted to make sure I caught you before you went home. I wanted to tell

you about the game plan I'd thought up. I'm so totally stupid."

"Don't be so hard on yourself. It's done. There's
nothing you can do about it now. Just be thankful
Amber is okay. The hospital says she's fine, right?"

"It's like I told you, she has a slight concussion. The
doc thinks she'll have a headache for a few days, but
that's it. The bummer part is she can't play any sports
for a week. That means the Dregs are double dead.
Why was I so dumb?"

"Hey, Joey," I wondered, "is there any rule in the
Mallory Trophy tournament about changing the people on a team after they've signed up?"

"I don't think so. Why?"

"If you can't play, you could still be our coach,
couldn't you?"

"I guess."

"And Amber could be the assistant coach and,
maybe, a cheerleader."

"What are you getting at, Stormy?"

"Why don't we find two new Dregs to take the
place of you and Amber."

"How?" he asked. "Who would want to be on our
team? I know how lucky I was to get you guys."

"I've got two people I have to phone," I said. "I'll
call you back."

Jonathan jumped at the chance. "You bet. I'll be
glad to take Joey's place. Thanks for thinking about
me. That's terrific, Stormy."

And after I told Loreeta how I was going to be
over in an hour to work on the science project, how
I had something important to ask her first, how the
Morton Mallory tournament worked, how Joey had

formed a team, how Joey had damaged himself and Amber and, finally, how the Dregs need a female player, how maybe she should be her old *image* for a day or two, her reaction was the same as Jonathan's, just as enthusiastic.

"Of course I would," she exclaimed. "Can I play goal?"

"You want to be the goalie?"

"That's my position," she stated. "I was on the school team, remember?"

"You're just what the doctor ordered."

13.

Please Remove Your Elbow From My Ear

We huddled around our net, moments before the start of the first game in the Morton Mallory floor hockey tournament at Taft Junior High School in Burlington, Vermont. The Dregs of the DT Dungeon, plus our last-minute imports, gave full attention to our coach and founder, Joey Floozeman.

In a way, I couldn't believe it was happening. I couldn't believe how proud I felt, proud to be part of the Dregs, proud to have these teammates as my friends. Everyone was so intense: Joey talking a mile a minute, Amber interjecting her advice with a wave of her finger, Jonathan face furrowed in concentration, Melvin, eyes half closed, breathing slowly, Loreeta carefully adjusting her leg pads, Dimps, looking part confused and part delighted, bouncing as much as Joey, anxious to start whatever was about to happen.

And I couldn't believe what was happening around me. The gym bleachers were packed with spectators, and they weren't just seventh graders. It seemed like half the kids in the school were jammed in. And half the teachers too. True to her word, Mrs. Ford sat in the front row. A smirking Mr. Waddell sat behind her.

On the top row of seats sat the Terminators, two dozen red jackets filled with jerks. I spotted Kevin the Barbarian. He was leaning against the wall, acting uninterested. *It must be tough to be cool all the time,* I thought.

It was intriguing to see that part of the audience was made up of the kids like me and Jonathan. The people everyone else called the weirdos, the geeks, the dweebs, the nerds, the lame-os or worse. A couple of them waved posters, DREGS RULE and DREGS ARE NUMERO UNO. It didn't take Sherlock Holmes to realize we'd been adopted as their team.

Sure the Screaming Eagles will beat us, I thought, *but we're going to give it a run. We're going to make it a game everyone will remember.*

"So one more time, team. What's the plan?" Joey asked.

"We stick one-to-one," Jonathan said.

"Stay with your check," I added. "Don't let them get a shot, and wait for the breaks."

This was Joey's strategy. He figured if we each stuck close to a player on the Screaming Eagles and concentrated on not letting him or her have a clear shot on the net, the luck of the game would fall our way and we'd peg a couple of goals while shutting them out.

"The best offense is a good defense," Amber said. "I heard that on TV once."

Mr. Woloski blew his whistle. "Let's get started."

Joey pointed to the bandage on his wrist. "This may stop me playing with you guys, but you're still my team." He pointed to his heart. "I'm with you a hundred percent in here."

"Me too," Amber said. Then to Jonathan's utter

amazement, she kissed him on the cheek. "Good luck, Jonathan."

Our coaches walked to the bleachers.

"Good luck, Jonathan," I teased.

"Let's kick some buttski," Melvin ordered. "Come on, Stormy."

Melvin and I headed for Mr. Woloski who was standing in the center of the gym. We were the forwards. That meant I was paired up against my *clarence* tormentor, Pierce Kobel. Melvin, of course, was opposite Dabny Paulty. The Flower Power formed their defense, matching up against Dimps and Jonathan. Loreeta was our goalie. Adon Kobel was theirs.

Pierce and I lined up for the face-off.

"You know the rules," Mr. Woloski said. "Two periods, fifteen minutes long each. Five minute break at half time. All penalties will be called. No body checking. Have fun."

He dropped the plastic puck and the game started.

Pierce won the draw and slipped the puck back to Tulip. She and Orchid broke out, charging into our end. It soon became obvious what the Screaming Eagles' game plan was. The moment Mr. Woloski turned to follow the play, Pierce slapped me across the shins with his plastic stick.

"Hey," I protested.

"Stay away from me, Stormy," he warned.

I wasn't prepared to take the *clarence* on Tuesday and I wasn't prepared to be slashed today. *Hit him back,* the little voice ordered.

This time I obeyed. I did. Across his rear end.

"Yeow!" Pierce protested.

The Dregs cheering section erupted into a loud round of applause.

Mr. Woloski twisted to find the cause of the celebration. But not in time. All he saw was Pierce rubbing the back of his sweats and me with an innocent expression etched on my face.

"This means war now," Pierce grunted.

Tulip entered our end, fed a pass to Dabny. He glanced up, saw Melvin looming nearby and quickly sent the puck to Orchid. She made a neat dipsydoodle around Dimps and lifted a wrist shot at the top left corner. Loreeta's trapper flew out and the plastic puck vanished into the leather.

Our fans howled their approval.

"Terrific save," I shouted.

Loreeta made another on the next play. And on the next. And on the one after that. In fact, she saved us from embarrassment eight times in the first five minutes of play.

"She's incredible," Jonathan said as we lined up for another face-off. "She's like a gymnast. If it wasn't for Loreeta, it would be five to zip already. We haven't even had a shot on their net."

I saw Adon Kobel, leaning on the Screaming Eagles' net. He appeared appropriately bored. Then I looked at Joey and Amber. Our coach and cheerleader looked appropriately concerned.

"Stick with 'em," Joey called. "Remember the game plan."

The problem with the game plan was, it wasn't working. The Flower Power and Pierce kept the puck away from Dabny. Since Melvin was shadowing him that kept the puck away from Melvin too. Our biggest asset was out of the game. Jonathan and I were doing so-so following Pierce and Tulip, but Orchid was running rings around Dimps. Dimps was trying to imitate what we were doing, but she was having as much trouble as she has with English.

To make matters worse, the Screaming Eagles' tactics were working perfectly. Every time Mr. Woloski was looking the other way, Jonathan, Dimps, or I would receive a slash or the butt end of a floor hockey stick. It got to the point where we were spooked, looking out for their fouls, rather than the puck.

Outside of Loreeta's outstanding saves, our fans had absolutely nothing to yell about. But the rest of the people watching us did. The friends of the Screaming Eagles were standing and praising their team with a continuous holler.

Loreeta's goalie skill couldn't keep us even forever. Pierce stood to the left of our net, watching the play. I stood next to him, my stick overlapping his, so he couldn't shoot if someone passed to him. While Mr. Woloski was watching Orchid deke around Dimps, Pierce leaned back and slammed his elbow into the side of my head.

"Ouch!" I yelled as a cauliflower of pain exploded around my ear. Then I let out a string of words I usually never say.

While I was complaining, Pierce ran at Loreeta, screaming an awesome rebel yell. She glanced at him for a fraction of a second, long enough for Orchid to fire a slap shot over her shoulder.

1–0 for them.

The Screaming Eagles clumped in a mass of high-fives and back slaps.

"What did I hear you say, Stormy?" Mr. Woloski demanded.

"Please remove your elbow from my ear," I answered.

"It didn't sound like that," he said. "Let's remember our sportsmanship."

I jogged up to Loreeta. "You're keeping us in the game."

"I should have had it," she moaned from behind the mask. "I shouldn't have fallen for that." Then after a moment, "What are you smiling at, Stormy?"

"I'm just thinking how cute you look in goalie pads."

"Get your mind on the game," she scolded. "We need some offense."

"My mind is on the game," I said, "but you're always on my mind too. I can't help it."

"Really?"

I nodded.

"Face-off, Stormy," Mr. Woloski called. "Get over here."

"What a nice thing to say." Loreeta's eyes sparkled through the mask's eye holes.

All right, I thought. I just said something that wasn't stupid.

"You don't move, you've got a delay-of-game penalty," Mr. Woloski warned.

I trotted over and lined up my stick with Pierce's. "A pretty lame effort, Dreg-meister," Pierce taunted. "When are you guys going to wake up? This is too easy."

"Maybe if you played fair, we'd be more even," I responded.

"Enough of that," Mr. Woloski said. "Concentrate on the game."

He dropped the puck and it bounced around on our

sticks for a few moments. By luck, it careened off my sneaker, spun in the air, and landed on the blade of Melvin's stick. The big guy nudged Dabny out of the way and rushed down the gym. Tulip and Orchid took one look at the raging beast and split up to let him pass. He ran full tilt, lips furled in concentration, and raised his stick to shoulder level. When he swung into his shot, the blade smacked the gym floor with an angry *thwack*. A fraction of a second later, the back of the Screaming Eagles' net exploded. Melvin had blasted the puck between Adon's legs. The Screaming Eagles' goalie hadn't even moved.

1–1.

You're lucky that wasn't six inches higher, Adon, I thought. That was a cup smasher.

Our fans stood up and bounced up and down on the bleachers. The noise thundered off the walls. Mrs. Ford and the teachers were instantly on their feet ordering everyone to sit.

"What an awesome shot, Melvin," I said. "Adon didn't even see it."

"Let's get another," he replied. "There's still twenty minutes left."

We lined up again.

"We woke up," I said to Pierce.

He mumbled something under his breath, so low neither Mr. Woloski nor I heard it. But whatever his comments, they definitely weren't polite.

Unfortunately, we quickly fell into our previous game style. The Screaming Eagles carried the play while we chased them around. It seemed like the puck was bouncing off a different part of Loreeta's body every ten seconds. With a minute left, Pierce deflected a point shot from Tulip. More by fluke than skill, the puck dribbled between Loreeta's legs.

2–1 for them.

I was glad when Mr. Woloski blew the half-time whistle. I was tired and out of breath. We were lucky to be down by only one goal. We had to change our game plan.

14.

A New Game Plan

"We need a new game plan," Joey said after he'd handed out the juice boxes.

"Like what?" Melvin asked.

"Something different," Amber reasoned. "Something they don't expect."

"I've got an idea," I said.

"What?" Loreeta wanted to know.

"We give them just that—something different," I explained. "We're forgetting where we came from. We made this team in detention. We formed it because we were in the DT Dungeon on Tuesday. We were the strange kids of the day, right?"

"I wasn't," Loreeta interjected.

"Me neither," Jonathan added.

"But you could have been," I went on. "Don't look like that. You know what I mean. We're together because we're different, so let's give them what we know best. Here we are trying to play like a regular team. But the Dregs aren't a normal team. So why don't we go out and do what we do best?"

"What's that?" Melvin asked.

"Whatever you want," I answered. "We still play one-on-one, but this time we do it creatively."

"I don't get it," Joey said.

"I'm saying we play like us—strangelike. We do

and say stupid things to throw them off. We do that all the time, don't we?"

"Speak for yourself," Amber said. "But I think I know what you're getting at, Stormy."

"It'll be fun," I reasoned. "And it may keep us in the game."

"Okay," Joey agreed reluctantly. "I don't understand. But as long as you do, Stormy, I'm willing to go along. So long as we don't look stupid, that is."

"I'm not worried about that," Amber said, "as long as we end up winning." Then she looked at Dimps. "Do you understand, Dimps?"

"Kes, I lick fur hooky," Dimps responded.

"I got a change to make before we start the second period," Joey announced. "I want to change the wingers. Melvin, you play on Pierce's side. Stormy, you go against Dabny."

"Why?" I puzzled.

"Pierce is a better player than Dabny," Joey coached. "If they're keeping Melvin out of the game by keeping the puck away from Dabny, let's make them take Pierce out of it too."

"Makes sense," Amber said.

"It does," Melvin agreed. "Smart thinking, coach."

Joey's grin stretched from Mercury to Pluto.

I finished the last of my Gatorade and tossed the box into the recycle bin. As we were walking back on the gym floor, Loreeta rested her trapper's mitt on my shoulder. "You look really sexy in your sweats," she said.

"I do?"

"I can't wait for tonight when we get to work on the science project again."

"You can't?"

I heard her pucker a kiss beneath the mask. What other motivation did I need?

This time Melvin lined up for the face-off. Pierce was paralyzed for a moment. Melvin stared into his face, then emitted a growl that originated from somewhere near the bottom of his lungs. So much for Pierce's slashes and butt ends, I figured.

Dabny looked smug. "Well, looks like I'm going to have a little fun after all."

"My Uncle Ernie used to play hockey," I whispered. "Did I ever tell you about him? He's the one who raises snakes."

"Everybody ready?" Mr. Woloski asked.

"His favorite is the Alberta viper. They live in western Canada."

"Why are you telling me this?" Dabny asked. "We're playing floor hockey."

"Because I'm crazy," I said. "Remember what I told you at lunchtime?"

I heard Mr. Woloski drop the puck and the *slap-slap* of hockey sticks. I didn't bother to join the play. Neither did Dabny. He was transfixed by my words. "Anyway, if the Alberta viper bites you, your body swells up four times its size and bursts open like a ripe tomato."

Dabny stood back a step. "What are you, Stormy? Nuts?"

I nodded. "That's what I've been trying to tell you. I've got an Alberta viper at home, Dabny. You want to pet it?"

"What are you—"

"Stormy!" Jonathan yelled.

I spun around in time to see the puck land at my feet. Quickly, I flipped it forward with my foot, picked it up with my stick, and ran toward Adon Kobel. I glanced to see who was with me. My only teammate was Dimps. She was running head-to-head with Orchid on the other side of the gym. It's too bad I couldn't get her to repeat Pierce's trick and have her scream at Adon.

Tulip moved over to cover me. If I could use her as a screen, I might be able to slip an easy shot past Adon. Wait a moment. Why couldn't I use Dimps?

"Hey, Dimps," I hollered. *"Unkos int kolvar."*

She looked at me and grinned. "Okay, Storkee."

Dimps cranked on the speed, barreling at the Screaming Eagles' net. I watched Adon's eyes flutter between her and me. I tried to move so I was behind Tulip. Adon's eyes fluttered again. Tulip shifted so I was blocked from Adon's view. Adon's vision locked on my rushing teammate. He must have been dumbfounded when he realized Dimps wasn't going to stop.

I slipped a gentle wrist shot over Tulip's stick. It entered the Screaming Eagles' goal a second before Dimps. Adon jumped high into the air as Dimps rolled underneath him. For a second time, my fellow Dreg ended up like a trapped fish.

Mr. Woloski ran over and helped her out. "What happened?" he asked. "Are you all right?"

Dimps was still grinning. "I lick fur hooky."

"That was a penalty," I said. "Orchid tripped Dimps."

"I did not," Orchid protested.

"I didn't see it," Mr. Woloski said.

"It's no goal," Adon asserted. "She was in the net when the puck went in."

He shook his head. "She tripped into the net after Stormy scored the goal."

"But I was trying to get out of the way," Adon complained.

"That's the rule," Mr. Woloski said. "It's a tie game."

2–2.

As soon as the gym teacher raised his hand to indicate a goal, our minicheering section went wild. The teachers had to stop people bouncing on the bleachers yet again.

"That's sort of like cheating," Jonathan said as we huddled to congratulate ourselves.

"And what Pierce did to Loreeta wasn't?" I said. "The cheap shots we've been taking all game isn't cheating? Maybe it's slightly less than legal, but it just evens things up. We can't use it again anyway. Mr. Woloski will know."

"New face-off," Mr. Woloski directed.

Our new tactics worked. I had Dabny completely psyched out. Every time I got close enough, I'd tell him about my Uncle Frank, who taught me how to play with axes, or my Aunt Susan, whose hobby was making homemade rocket launchers. He may not have believed me, but I had him wondering if I was dangerous or not.

Melvin made a big deal about huffing and puffing, snarling and growling as if he were really angry. Pierce didn't want to go near him. The Flower Power were thrown off by Jonathan's constant requests that they should go dancing with him. Our *weirdness* evened the sides. We were matched teams.

We played end to end for the next ten minutes. Loreeta was spectacular in our net. She stopped everything they pounded at her. In the other goal, Adon kept the Screaming Eagles in the game. It could go either way.

We blew it with thirty seconds left to play.

Melvin and I were pressing in the Screaming Eagles' end of the gym. And Dimps was flying around, way out of position, but still trying to help out. I thought about dropping back to cover defense for Dimps, but we were getting some decent shots. In fact, I had a half-empty net when Tulip snatched the puck off my stick and flipped it up the gym to Dabny.

The big guy took off, faster than I thought he could run, rolling toward Loreeta. Pierce was running with him. The only person back was Jonathan. A two on one. I'd just handed the Screaming Eagles a goal.

Jonathan backpedaled, trying to stay between the Screaming Eagles' forwards. He'd have to commit in a second—to go after Dabny and let Paulty pass it over to Pierce for a clear shot, or cover Pierce, leaving Dabny with a breakaway. Either way was a no-win situation.

But then Jonathan pulled an amazing stunt. He dropped his stick and began to dance. Right there, in the middle of the game, in the middle of the gym, he started dancing. He raised his hands above his head and snapped his fingers, slapping his sneakers on the floor in a Latin rhythm.

"Olé," Jonathan called. "Olé!"

Poor old Dabny and Pierce. All period, they'd been bombarded by my chatter and Melvin's grunts. Now the defense was doing a tango in the middle of their scoring chance. It was enough to make them stop for a moment, shake their heads, and wonder, Why has the world suddenly gone crazy?

A moment was all Dimps needed.

She'd raced after the Screaming Eagles' forwards. When Dabny hesitated, she was there to poke-check the puck. Once the plastic disk was on her stick, she rifled a pass to Melvin. All of a sudden, we were running the other way. I darted for the Screaming Eagles' net. My plan was to screen Adon, and Melvin could pop a goal with me blocking the goalie's view. If I couldn't do that, I was hoping for a rebound.

Of course, I didn't see what happened because I was facing the net. Jonathan told me it was probably one of the most awesome plays he's ever seen. Personally, I find it kind of ridiculous.

I'd positioned myself in front of Adon. Melvin geared up and released a vicious slap shot. A shot that by Jonathan's estimate was, "A good foot high of the net." Which was approximately the same altitude as the side of my head. I felt the *crack* more than heard it. My eyes filled with little static bursts. I saw the puck sail under Adon's armpit as I heard Mr. Woloski blowing the whistle for the end of the game.

I didn't pass out, but I did feel a sudden urge to lie down on the floor. The next scene I focused on was a herd of people standing above me. The electric bursts were still there, but rapidly fading. I looked up at Mr. Woloski's concerned face and the faces of the Dregs and Screaming Eagles. The sound of spectators clomping on gym bleachers vibrated the gym floor.

"How many fingers do you see, Stormy?" Mr. Woloski held his hand in front of my face.

"Two," I answered.

He appeared relieved.

"Did the goal count?" I wanted to know.

"You scored," Jonathan said. "We won the game." 3–2 for the Dregs.

There was only one thing left to do.

"Help me up," I said. I reached out my arm for support and grabbed hold of Pierce Kobel's sweatpants. With a coordinated tug, I yanked them down.

A perfect *clarence*.

15.

And Proud of It

Two weeks later, I was sitting in the DT Dungeon with Dimps. There was no one else in the room. Amber was all caught up on her science, thanks to a lot of help from Jonathan. Mr. Waddell was on a smoke break.

"You know, Dimps, I still find it hard to believe my name is engraved on the Morton Mallory Trophy. I never thought anything like that would happen. Ever. Funny how one day can change your whole life. A few days actually, but if Pierce hadn't *clarenced* me and Joey wasn't in the Dungeon, if we all hadn't been in the Dungeon, if Jonathan hadn't given me the courage to call Loreeta and so on."

"I peg my bardon, Storkee."

"Winning the floor hockey tournament wasn't easy, was it?" I continued. "We played some tough teams. I mean two of the games went into overtime. But whenever we were down or in a tough spot, that old Dreg luck popped up, didn't it, and we managed to pull out a victory. You got better so fast. And we never resorted to the tactics we used against the Screaming Eagles, but the personality of our *difference* was always there, wasn't it?"

"I peg your bardon."

"Wasn't it awesome the way our cheering section

got louder and larger with each game? Both the students and the teachers. Even the half of the school who didn't like us treated us with something like respect.

"And I find it amazing the way the Dregs have paired up. Loreeta and me, of course. Wasn't it neat the way Amber let Joey out of his promise to do her science project when she and Jonathan agreed to work on one together. And you and Melvin? Wow."

"I lick Melkin."

"Yeah. Whatever. Isn't it incredible how Joey has gotten so friendly with that girl in eighth grade, Norma Fitts? Do you know that Norma collects bugs? 'It's a fascinating hobby,' Joey told me. 'Who couldn't like a girl who collects bugs?' I considered Norma an honorary Dreg right away.

"And don't forget the Terminators. Wasn't it great how Amber backed up Jonathan's story to the police? Kevin has certainly kept a low profile since that happened, hasn't he? Jonathan is determined to go to juvenile court about the assault.

"It was Jonathan's courage that helped me go to Mrs. Ford with Amber to discuss our feelings about Mr. Waddell. The assistant principal must have spoken to him. Have you noticed how much less obnoxious he's been the last little while?"

"I peg your pardon."

"Do you know it was me who finked the Terminators' insurance plan to Mrs. Ford? Why wasn't I brave enough to do that months ago? She stopped it fast, didn't she? I love the fact that the Terminators aren't allowed to wear their jackets to school anymore.

"And my brother Brandon? I'm so proud of him.

He certainly doesn't have to worry about Darry Paulty anymore. His stories about his crazy relatives were even more effective than mine. In fact, Darry ran home crying because he thought our Uncle Igor was a vampire who was going to visit him every night."

"I beg your pardon, Stormy."

"I now believe there's hope for all the kids like me. . . . Huh? What did you just say?"

"I beg your pardon, Stormy," Dimps repeated.

"You said it right. You got it right, Dimps. Way to go."

Her face beamed.

Mr. Waddell strode into the room. "I heard you talking down the hall. You'd better have a good explanation. You know the rules of the Dungeon."

Dimp's face furrowed in concentration for several moments. Then, speaking slowly, she said, "I'm a Dreg and I am proud of it."

MARTYN GODFREY is an ex-junior high teacher who wrote his first book on a dare by one of his students. Since that time, he has written nearly thirty books for young people. Many of the humorous incidents in his stories originate from his fan mail. "I get lots of letters from young people," he explains. "Most of them tell me of a funny experience. It's great reading about the silly things that happen to people." Besides writing, Martyn's hobbies include growing older and collecting comic books.